GOT IT BAD

BAD BOYS OF THE BAYOU

ERIN NICHOLAS

ISBN: 978-1-952280-51-1
Cover Design: Najla Qamber, Qamber Designs

AUTHOR'S NOTE

I've been published for over a decade and have written a lot of books in that time. I actually don't know how many. I've counted a few times before but there are short stories and novellas, bonus material, things that have gone out of print, or been re-worked… and I don't know how to count all of that. I usually say, "over fifty books" and figure that's safe.

But in all of that vagueness there are a few things that have become what I call my "orphans" over the years. Books and stories that don't really *belong* anywhere specific anymore. I was first published with Samhain Publishing which has since closed its doors, and all of those books came back to me, including stand-alone stories that didn't connect with anything else. I've also had some really amazing opportunities to participate in various projects and events and series for which I've written a story (or stories) and I've enjoyed them all! But projects end, and opportunities shift. So, over the years, projects, series, and publishers have come and gone. But the stories are still alive and well. They just don't really *fit* anywhere.

So I finally decided that I needed to give them a home. And a new chance to meet readers! They needed a new place to live. But I needed to put them all together and give them a connection to one another since they didn't have other connections.

And, where else would I make this new home than Louisiana?

Now I couldn't just bring these people (some of whom I've known since before I was published!) to Autre, the home of my other Louisiana books. They don't quite fit there. They have a different vibe. They came from a little different Erin Nicholas. Not totally different, of course. My voice and style have always been pretty consistent.

But these stories are a little grittier. More emotional. The people have a little more baggage than the Boys (and girls) of the Bayou or the people of Boys of the Bayou Gone Wild. They're also a little dirtier. There's always open-door sex scenes in my books, but in Bad, Louisiana, there are just more of them. These books just have a little different feel. And they needed their own home. Their own place to live and be what they are rather than trying to fit into something else.

So, I present to you Bad, Louisiana. A collection of books that have existed in Erin Nicholas world for a long time but have been rewritten and edited to fit together in a new town, with some new friends, for a second chance to meet readers and bring even more love stories to the Louisiana bayou!

I hope you enjoy them as much as I did when I first wrote them and loved them again going back for this reimagining.

If you're a long-time reader and are "afraid" that you might have read these books before, you can check out the original titles and more information here: https://bit.ly/BadBoys-ThenNow

WELCOME TO BAD, LOUISIANA!

These boys are only called "bad" because of their hometown…

Yeah, right.

I've been to Bad several times over the years and it always makes me smile. The town itself has an interesting history. It was originally, and very briefly, settled by a bunch of Germans. Did you know that Germans use "bad" in town names to denote a spa town? Yep, that's a thing.

So, I guess in this case, there was a small hot spring outside of town and the settlers claimed that made it a spa town in the new frontier. They named the town Bad Salzuflen and they'd hoped it would attract even more settlers. Particularly of the young and female persuasion.

But, unfortunately, the 'hot spring' was actually just a particularly marshy area (no one knows why it was so much warmer… or at least they're not saying) and then, before they could figure out what to do about that, the French showed up and ran the Germans out.

Well, after that no one could pronounce or spell Bad Salzuflen, but they didn't really want to go to the trouble of renaming the whole thing, so they just dropped the Salzuflen, painted over that part of the welcome sign, and the town decided to lean into the whole *Bad* thing. Especially in more modern times.

Seriously. The hair salon is called *Bad Hair Day?* (yes with a question mark so that when they answer the phone it's, "Bad hair day?" and you say, "Yes", and they say, "Come on down and let us fix it!" And there's so much more.

Here's a quick list:
Bad Habit—coffeeshop
Bad Brakes—auto mechanic shop
Bad Brews—bar and restaurant
The Bad Egg—diner/cafe
Bad Gas—gas station and convenience store
Bad Faith Community Church—local church
Bad Hair Day?—hair salon
The Bad Place—the physical therapy clinic
Bad Medicine—the medical clinic
Bad Memories—community center

Instead of fighting it and letting everyone else mock them, the citizens decided to have some fun with it. And hey, they sell a lot of merch (like *I got Bad Gas on my roadtrip* travel mugs and *I've been to The Bad Place and survived* t-shirts) and no one ever forgets a trip to Bad!

So come on in and have some fun! It really will be a *good* time!

THE SERIES

You can read the Bad Boys of the Bayou in any order!

The Best Bad Boy: (Jase and Priscilla)
A bad boy-good girl, small town romance

Bad Medicine: (Brooke and Nick)
A hot boss, medical, small town romance

Bad Influence: (Marc and Sabrina)
An enemies to lovers, road trip / stuck together, small town
romance

Bad Taste in Men: (Luke and Bailey)
A friends to lovers, gettin'-her-groove back, small town romance

Not Such a Bad Guy: (Regan and Christopher)
A one-night-stand, mistaken identity, small town romance

Return of the Bad Boy: (Jackson and Annabelle)
A bad boy-good girl, fake relationship, small town romance

Bad Behavior: (Carter and Lacey)
A bad boy-good girl, second chance small town romance

Got It Bad: (Nolan and Randi)
A nerd-tomboy, opposites attract, small town romance

GOT IT BAD

You can take the boy away from the bayou, but you can't take the love for sexy small town girls out of the boy. Evidently.

Nolan Winters left his hometown after high school, wanting bigger things than Bad, Louisiana could offer. Years later, he's a popular journalist, reporting stories that stir him, and also a bestselling author, working on his second book—a biography about one of Louisiana's most beloved football coaches, Bad's very own Coach Karr. Now Nolan's finding himself home a lot more often. For research. Yeah. That's the story he's sticking to. He's not coming home for sexy, sweet local mechanic, Miranda Doyle. Nope. Not at all.

Randi's a born-and-bred Bad girl, more than content to stay there forever. Football, steady work, football, family and friends, football...her small hometown has everything she needs. And lately, something she wants—Nolan Winters. Never much of an athlete, he's asked football fanatic Randi for help on the ins and outs of football for his new book about Coach. It isn't long before Randi would rather help the hot nerd in and out of other things...like her bedroom, and definitely his clothes.

She's a small-town, C-average ex-cheerleader. He's a big-city, A-plus bookworm. Their differences could keep their engines running hot...or steer them straight toward a crash and burn.

PROLOGUE

FIVE MONTHS *ago*

Everyone was so freaking *happy* she thought she might be sick.

Miranda Doyle tipped her beer back and took a long swig. The party was going strong and Randi loved nothing more than a good party. Her favorite people were all here and everyone was dancing, drinking and laughing.

And she wanted to be *anywhere* else.

The party was celebrating the first game of the football season and the high school naming the football field after their beloved, longtime coach, Davis Karr. Randi loved Coach. He'd been an advisor and confidant for her in the past, just like he had for every other kid even remotely associated with his boys, the football teams of the thirty-some years he'd been coaching. Randi had been the head cheerleader both her junior and senior years, so she'd had time to hang out with Coach. She was thrilled that they'd honored him that way, thrilled that the team had won the big game against Autre tonight, and thrilled to see her friends and classmates having such a great time.

She sighed and lifted her heavy hair off the back of her neck.

It was a beautiful September night in Louisiana, but inside the new community center filled with people celebrating Coach Davis Karr's long and influential career, it was hot.

Especially when she looked at her best friend Annabelle dancing with her fiancé Jackson, or Regan, who was in the corner with her new boyfriend, Christopher. Everyone was falling in love. Except for her.

Par for the course.

But it was getting old.

She drained her beer and tried to decide if she wanted another one.

She scanned the bottles behind the bar where the community center manager Jase, and his girlfriend Priscilla, the downtown bar owner, Marc, and his best friend, Luke, and *his* girlfriend Bailey, were all scrambling to keep up with the thirsty partygoers. Her eyes went right on past the top-shelf tequila—that she *really* wanted—and to the dance floor, where the new girl, Lacey, was being swung around the hardwood by Nolan Winters.

Quiet, sophisticated, bookworm Nolan Winters. Who was now wearing denim jeans that were clearly several washings past new as they molded to a very nice backside. And front side, for that matter. The blue t-shirt he wore showed off shoulders and a chest that Randi had, in fact, been impressed with before, and his feet moved through the dance steps like the born-and-bred Louisiana boy that he was.

To anyone looking on—and clearly to the new girl, Lacey—Nolan fit right in with the other country boys in the barn, swigging beer and singing along to every song the live band, The Locals, cranked out. But the people who had gone to high school with him knew better.

Nolan had spent most of his time in the library and the tiny office of the school newspaper, rather than at the river drinking beer or skinny dipping. He'd always been quiet, reserved—at least compared to the live-large Bad boys like Jackson Brady and Carter Shaw and the rest. But it hadn't been in a shy way or like he didn't fit in. It had been as though he'd been observing, taking it all in, making notes.

And now he was an award-winning journalist. Go figure.

But as Randi eyed his two-step—and the fit of his jeans—she couldn't believe it was the same guy.

He'd come into his own, as her mother would say.

She supposed ten years could do that to a guy. As could accomplishing all his career goals, writing a best-selling book, and then getting a huge New York publishing deal for another one. This time he was writing it about Coach Karr and his influence on football, small-town Louisiana, and the boys that had played for him.

She knew he was being flown to New York on a regular basis and had gotten a "scandalous" amount of money as an advance on his book.

She even knew that he'd worn a dark gray pinstriped suit to meet with his new publisher for the first time.

God bless—and curse—the grapevine in Bad, Louisiana.

Randi's mother got her hair done downtown once a month at Bad Hair Day?, had coffee at Bad Habit every Tuesday and Thursday morning, played poker with her friends every Friday night, and went to Bible study at Bad Faith Community Church every Wednesday afternoon.

There was nothing that anyone who had ever lived in Bad, Louisiana, could do that Randi wouldn't hear about.

Though, she could admit, she'd heard just as much about Nolan from her own customers. She was the co-owner of Bad Brakes, the town's only auto repair shop with her friend Luke Hamilton, making her one of two mechanics in town. It was rare for the men to know something the ladies didn't—most of them got the gossip from their wives—but every once in a while they'd repeat a detail the women had left out.

Though Randi had no idea why, details about Nolan stuck in her head, so she knew a lot of things about Nolan Winters that she didn't really mean to.

But she couldn't disagree with the assessment that he had come into his own. And, not for the first time, she wondered if she'd come into *her* own yet. That seemed like something someone should know about themselves.

"Two shots of Patron and another Bud Light," Randi told Bailey.

Bailey gave her a grin as she grabbed the bottle. "I could just make one shot a double."

Ah, so it was obvious she was drinking alone. "Great. Make them both doubles."

"Both of them?" Bailey asked, eyebrows up.

"Unless you can make triples."

Bailey laughed and poured. And emptied the bottle.

Well, even if the damned shot glasses were bigger, she would have been out of luck. Typical. She wanted to get wasted, but there wasn't enough tequila. Bailey pushed the shots across the makeshift bar and opened her mouth to say something, but someone called out that they were in need of vodka STAT.

"You good?" Bailey asked.

Nope. Lonely, a little horny, and not nearly drunk enough.

"This will help," Randi said, toasting her with one of the shots. "Go deal with the vodka emergency." Randi had been there too.

She looked down at the two shots in her hands and sighed. These would either make tonight a lot better.

Or a lot worse.

But it was the unknown that made her tip the first back and then grab her beer and the other shot as she headed for the back door of the building and some cooler air.

Bring on the adventure, she thought. Then giggled. Because this was Bad. Despite it's name, nothing unexpected ever happened here.

Just the way she liked it.

———

Nolan left Lacey with Annabelle and Jackson. He'd brought her to the party as a favor to his friend, and her boyfriend, Carter. Carter was the town cop and had needed to make sure that everything in town was settled and safe after the Renegades' big win over Autre, but he'd be here soon enough.

And though Lacey was emotional tonight, and Nolan sensed something brewing with her and Carter, he couldn't ignore that Miranda Doyle had just slipped out the back of the barn. Alone. And at least a little tipsy and probably more like drunk. He couldn't let her go wandering around in the dark by herself and he definitely couldn't let her get into her car.

He'd been watching her all night. He guessed he wasn't the only guy in the room doing so. She was gorgeous, as always. Her dark hair fell nearly to her mid-back, her long legs were bare beneath the hem of the short dress she wore, and her five-foot-eight was now five-foot-ten with the black combat boots on her feet.

He was watching her because whenever Randi Doyle was within a city block of him, he couldn't help it. Everyone else was probably watching her because she didn't look like the usual Randi. This was going-out Randi. Or Sunday-church Randi. Her hair was down, she had a dress on, belted at the waist with a thick black belt and big sparkly buckle, and had jewelry on around her neck and wrists. It was all a far cry from the dirty overalls, ponytail, and work boots she spent most days in at Bad Brakes as one of the only mechanics in town.

Okay, the boots were similar. But these black leather boots weren't covered in motor oil. These were laced up past her ankle but had a little heel and drew attention to lot of smooth bare skin between the top of the leather and the hem of her skirt.

It was the crazy contrast between the weekday Randi who drank pots of black coffee, swore like a trucker, and could put a transmission together faster than anyone in the parish, and the sexy girl who could rock a skirt, that made her so fascinating to most of the men around here.

A girl who was low maintenance enough to get motor oil under her nails and didn't get offended by locker-room humor, but who could wear dresses that made a man think very dirty thoughts while still being perfectly comfortable taking her to meet his mama at Sunday dinner. That was Miranda Magnolia Doyle.

And all of it made Nolan feel pretty smug.

He'd noticed all of this about Randi way back.

Watching Randi Doyle was one of his favorite pastimes. It had certainly made football season go faster for him with her as a cheerleader.

He'd never been that into football, but he'd liked the guys on the team, loved Coach Karr, loved the way football fever swept over the town every fall and united everyone who wore the black and silver. And Randi.

Yes, football had definitely had a few high points for him, in spite of not having one single urge to put on pads and hit the turf himself.

Nolan weaved his way through the crowd. Everyone had turned out, it seemed. Not just because of the big win and the gorgeous early September night but because of Coach. Nolan should be observing the party and taking time to talk to a few people for his new book.

Later. After he checked on Randi.

She'd done one shot and had taken the other and a third beer with her outside. Not to mention she'd been wearing an expression that had looked sad, pissed off, and thoughtful all at the same time for the past hour.

Nolan stepped out of the back door into the night. The light from the party spilled out onto the back patio of Bad Memories, the newly named community center that had once been a strip club/ barbecue joint called The Pork and Peach. Bad Memories maybe wasn't a much better name. But it was funny. At least to a big section of the people who lived in Bad. It wasn't that the memories would automatically be *bad* of course, but the memories would be *from* Bad. It had definitely made Nolan chuckle when he'd heard it.

That was how all the business names in his hometown went. Bad Gas was the convenience store which was, of course, where people got gas for their vehicles in Bad. But they also sold a ton of travel mugs that said *I got Bad Gas in Louisiana*. The town newspaper was *The Bad News*. Because…it was the news from Bad. It went on and on, up and down Main Street. The town loved to laugh at themselves.

With the exception of Bad Faith Community Church. Pastor Williams did *not* find that one particularly funny.

The stone patio behind Bad Memories stretched for several yards and held a number of tables and chairs. There were lights strung over the patio, making it easy for Nolan to see that Randi wasn't the only one who had slipped out.

There was a cluster of guys off to one side, talking and laughing. They lifted their hands in greeting and he gave them a wave. There were a few couples as well. Some were just talking, others were doing a little more. When his first scan of the immediate area didn't reveal Randi anywhere, he rounded the corner of the building and heard a female moan. He quickly reversed direction.

Finally he saw her. There was dirt and grass for several more yards beyond the patio before the taller grasses grew up and the ground got marshier on the way to the bayou. She was perched on the top of the wooden railing that separated the backyard of the community center from the field. She was looking out over the darkness, twinkling with lightning bugs, and lifting a beer bottle to her lips.

"Randi?"

He said it softly, trying not to startle her. But it didn't work. She gasped and started to turn, and the combination of the scare, the narrow piece of wood she was sitting on and the tequila apparently all hit at once. He reached her just as she started to pitch forward. He grabbed her by her belt and hauled her back up onto the fence.

For a second she just breathed. Then she twisted her head to look at him. "Holy shit, that was impressive."

He gave her a grin. "Thank God for country girls who wear big-ass belts."

She laughed. "Didn't even spill a drop of beer."

"Amazing," he said dryly.

"Nolan Winters, what are you doin' out here?" she asked, squinting at him in the dark.

"Checking on you."

"On me?" She wrinkled her nose. "Why?"

"Well, I can't dance with you out here. I went to look for you inside but you'd disappeared."

No sense in letting her know that he knew every move she'd made since she'd walked into the party. That sounded creepy.

"You wanted to dance with me?"

"Of course." Who the fuck *wouldn't* want to dance with her?

"You and Lacey were dancing."

Was there a twinge of jealousy in her voice? No. Nolan immediately shook his head. There was no way Randi was jealous of another girl dancing with him. There had never been anything between him and Randi, ever, but friendship. If she'd wanted him, she could have had him. For anything. Boyfriend, booty call, slave, minion.

"Lacey and I are just friends," he told her. "She's with Carter."

"Oh, good," Randi said—then her eyes widened as if she hadn't meant to say that.

Nolan wasn't sure he'd ever heard anything better from her.

He was a little embarrassed *now* about how infatuated he'd been with her, and he no longer felt willing to give her a kidney just for a smile, but he was still...enamored. Possibly more so now than ever, in some ways. Because now he knew what he'd been missing as a nerd who liked books better than people.

He still, generally, liked books better than people. But he did *not* like books better than sex.

Definitely not.

And if he had a fantasy girl, it was the one sitting drunkenly on a fence on the outskirts of Bad, Louisiana.

For fuck's sake.

Nolan shook his head. You could take the boy out of the small hick Louisiana town, but you couldn't take his love for small town Louisiana girls out of the boy. Apparently.

It was something he'd been trying to kick for years.

But sophisticated, polished city chicks just didn't do it for him.

Girls who wore jeans and used fuck as a noun, verb, adjective and adverb, who liked to get dirty—whether it was actual, good old dirt, or naughty in a backseat, or with wrenches and grease —who drank tequila, and loved football, and would rather be outside, rain or shine, than indoors did it for him. No matter what he did to try to kick the addiction.

He made a good show of liking things more cultured. He'd developed a taste for wine and he actually liked Broadway. Most of it. He could name all the courses of a seven-course meal and he really did like tailored suits. He'd always been an avid reader and a connoisseur of current events and politics, so he could hold his own in conversations with the people he met at New York publishing parties, but he had actually found himself missing talk about the weather and football—two of the main topics of almost any conversation in Louisiana.

So, he was a gentleman. Guys in Louisiana were raised to be, and his mother, a single mom who was very bitter about being single, had impressed upon him how important it was to treat women well. But now he knew how to be smooth and classy too.

But instead of doing that, and letting Randi off the hook for her comment, he said, "Good, huh? Why's that?"

Randi turned her attention back on the view in front of her.

Nolan moved in to rest his forearms on the top of the fence and put a foot up on the bottom railing.

"Well, I heard she was engaged to Garrett Dunn before he died."

Garrett was also a Bad boy. He'd been a cop in Baton Rouge and had been killed in the line of duty. Nolan nodded. "She was. But she and Carter were very good friends while she was with Garrett and their feelings grew into more."

Randi seemed to be thinking about that as she took a long draw of her beer.

"Okay," she said after a moment. She swung her legs over the fence, hopped to the ground, wobbled slightly, and then straightened to face him with a big smile.

"Okay what?" he asked, resisting the urge to grab her to be sure she stayed upright. Then he wondered why he'd resisted. It was a great excuse to touch her.

"You can dance with me."

But that was an even better excuse to touch her. He moved in closer. "Okay."

Randi started to step past him, but he caught her arm. She looked up in surprise.

"Out here," he said.

"Thought you said you couldn't dance with me out here?"

The music drifted out this far. It was soft but clear. And it was dark. And they were alone. Out here was definitely his choice. "Well, might as well stay here. There's no tequila left in there," he said, pulling her around in front of him and taking her hand in his as he settled the other on her lower back.

She put a hand on his shoulder, but she was studying his face rather than moving her feet.

Nolan didn't think they'd ever stood this close to one another before. They'd definitely never stood this close when it was just the two of them. He and Randi had mostly socialized with one another while in groups. They had several friends in common, mostly people connected to the football program—players,

GOT IT BAD   11

cheerleaders and avid fans—so they'd been at parties together
and such in high school, and since. A football occasion never
went by without someone in Bad throwing a party. Whether it
was a home game for the Renegades, the Super Bowl, or any
football event in between, there was a social event happening in
Bad. But they had rarely even had a conversation just between
the two of them. He could recall maybe half a dozen over the
years. And they'd all been extremely awkward.

Nolan had always thought it was because they had very little
in common. He had always been self-conscious about what he
was saying, if he was getting the football jargon right, if his
breath smelled, if he looked the part of the dork with a crush.

But now that he thought back on it with ten years of matura-
tion, Randi had seemed nervous, or fidgety, or something
around him too. And every time they'd talked, something
strange had happened.

Once they'd been talking, stiltedly, about geometry class.
Suddenly she'd asked if he wanted to see her tattoo. She'd
pulled her jeans down on one side and showed him the ladybug
tattoo on her left hip. He'd had dirty dreams about that for two
weeks afterward.

Then there had been the time they'd been at a party chatting
by the snack table about the trouble Jackson had gotten into with
one of their teachers. Jackson had been caught having sex with
their new young teacher and had been kicked off the football
team. There had come an awkward pause in the conversation.
Randi had dunked a chip in dip and some of the dip had
dropped onto the upper curve of her right breast—he could still
remember the exact spot. She'd wiped the drip up with the tip of
her finger and as she licked it off, her eyes had met Nolan's. And
she'd blurted, "My peach body powder actually tastes like
peaches."

He'd had dirty dreams about peaches dunked in ranch after
that.

There was another time when she'd said something about

having poison ivy on her butt and thighs was the most miserable she'd ever been, and the time she'd confessed that she and two of her friends slept naked outside one summer night. He couldn't remember what had prompted either of those admissions, or if they were even somehow connected, because Randi saying the word "naked" pretty much sucked everything else out of his mind.

Their one-on-ones were always a little bizarre. It was probably no wonder they'd both seemed to avoid conversations with one another.

Her tongue darted out to nervously wet her lips, and he found himself mesmerized by the pink tip and the shininess it left behind.

She reached for the fence and the other shot glass he hadn't noticed until now. She brought it to her mouth and, with her eyes locked on his, she shot it back. She swallowed, set the glass back on the fence, and stepped closer to him.

"Sorry about drinking all the tequila," she finally said. "Maybe I can share."

And suddenly Nolan felt her hand at the back of his head, drawing him down, and then her warm, soft lips against his.

Surprise and desire battled to be the primary emotion coursing through his body.

But then her tongue slid along *his* bottom lip and desire won hands down.

Nolan opened his mouth as both of his hands dropped to her hips and brought her body against his. He definitely tasted the tequila. And a spicy sweetness that was all Randi—and all he'd ever wanted.

Randi gave a little moan as his hands slid from her hips to her ass. He was going to lose his mind. But it was going to be a very nice trip to crazy.

Her fingers curled into his hair as her other hand fisted the front of his shirt. She arched closer and Nolan took over the kiss. He stroked her tongue hungrily, then gentled things, kissing her softly, nipping at her bottom lip before again pressing against her tongue, trying to drink her in.

He felt her leg wrap around his, and he couldn't help but drop his hand from her ass to the back of her thigh below the hem of her short dress. Her skin was like silk, and while he might not give a kidney for a smile, he'd definitely give one away for the chance to lick her right there.

And she'd been right about sharing the tequila this way. He was absolutely feeling tipsy now. But it was that thought that made him lift his head. As much as he'd love to make out with Randi for another solid hour or so out here, he wouldn't do it with her when she was drunk.

She stared up at him, breathing fast. Nolan also had to draw in two or three gulps of oxygen before he could speak.

"Thanks for the taste," he said.

She pressed her lips together, then asked, "You sure you got enough?"

He almost groaned. He wasn't sure there would ever be such a thing as enough with her. "My head's spinning," he told her. "And I've got to drive."

Randi let him go and stepped back. For a second, Nolan kicked himself. What the fuck was he doing? Turning her down for more of *that*? This was Miranda Doyle. He might never get another shot. But he didn't want a drunken shot. He wanted her fully with him and he wanted her to remember it for a very long time afterward.

Like he would.

She wet her lips again, watching him. "I have more tequila back at my place," she said. "But I don't have any shot glasses. We might have to do body shots instead."

Jesus. Nolan thought his heart skipped a beat there. Talk about the most tempting thing he'd ever heard in his life.

It didn't matter how many women he'd been with. Simply kissing Randi had just obliterated the taste of any other woman from his mind. Of course, it had been a hell of a kiss and was fueled by the fact that he'd dreamed of it for a long, long time. And it had been even better than anything his imagination had come up with. He'd never shoot Patron without thinking of her —and probably getting hard—again.

Which meant that the only time he should really do tequila shots would be *with* her. Like right now.

But no. She was drunk.

"I'll take you home," he told her. "But I can't stay."

She frowned. "I promise not to talk."

Nolan paused at that. She promised not to talk? What did that mean? "Randi—"

"Have you done body shots before?" she asked. She moved in closer and put a hand on his chest. "You lick the salt off my neck, suck the tequila out of my belly button, and then take the lime from my mouth."

Nolan cleared his throat. He knew the basics, had seen it done, but had never done it himself. Suddenly he wanted nothing more in the entire world than to suck tequila from her belly button.

"Or I could put the lime right here." She ran her finger from her collarbone to the glorious dip between her breasts. "And really, you can lick the salt from wherever you want to."

That list was embarrassingly long.

"Randi, if you weren't drunk, I'd take you up on all of that in a New York minute, but—"

Her brows slammed together and she pushed him back. She ran a hand through her hair. "Yeah, okay, whatever. I guess women in New York don't put limes between their breasts, right?"

She stepped around him and stomped toward the community center.

It took Nolan another minute to follow. What had that been about? He hadn't mentioned New York on purpose, it was just an expression.

He didn't catch up with her until she was standing in front of her best friend, Annabelle, and her boyfriend Jackson.

"Can you take me home?" Randi asked Annabelle before Nolan could say anything.

Annabelle's gaze went to Nolan. "Of course," she told Randi. "You ready now?"

"Yes," Randi said firmly.

"I can take you," Nolan said from behind her.

Randi swung around so fast that she wobbled. He didn't resist this time. He reached out and took her arm, keeping her upright and bringing her closer.

"I'm fine," Randi said. But she didn't try to shake his hold off.

"How about that dance?" he asked. He wanted a chance to talk to her, to make sure she understood that he wasn't rejecting her because he didn't want her.

And what universe was this anyway, where *he* was reassuring Randi Doyle that he wanted her?

"I don't want to dance," she told him. "I want to go home. Alone."

"Nolan," Jackson said, stepping forward. "We've got her."

"I just…" Nolan looked down at Randi and let go of her arm. "I just want her to wake up tomorrow feeling good."

With no regrets. Like doing body shots—and more—with him because she'd been drunk and melancholy.

"I'll be sure she gets ibuprofen and lots of water before bed," Annabelle said, wrapping her arm around Randi's waist.

Yeah, ibuprofen and water, that was a much better solution than giving her what *he* wanted to give her before bed. And in bed. And in the middle of the night. But part of him couldn't shake the feeling that if what she most needed was ibuprofen, then he wanted to be the one providing that too.

"Thanks," he said, stepping back.

Annabelle and Randi turned toward the front of the barn and Jackson moved to follow, but he paused and looked at Nolan.

"Everything okay with the two of you?"

Nolan gave a humorless laugh. "Of course." Then he said the main thing that mattered at that moment. "There's not a two of us anyway."

Jackson didn't reply to that, but he clapped Nolan on the shoulder and then followed the girls out to where the cars were parked all over the grass in front of the barn.

"You look sad."

He looked down. Lacey. With Annabelle and Jackson taking Randi home, she was alone again until Carter got there.

"Dance with me," he said. Dancing with a beautiful woman was always a good idea. Even if she wasn't *his* beautiful woman.

As he took Lacey into his arms, his gaze went to the barn door where Randi had disappeared. It was the stupidest thing to ever cross his mind but *his woman* made him think of Randi, and the idea of her doing body shots with anyone else, ever, made him want to kill someone.

Him. A guy who had never even punched another guy. But yeah, the idea of someone else's mouth on her body made him see red.

"Hey, ow."

He looked down and realized he'd been squeezing Lacey's hand tightly.

"Jesus, sorry." He let go and shoved a hand through his hair.

"It's okay," she said. "You seem riled up."

Just then something caught his eye at the front of the barn. Carter was finally here. And he looked more riled up than Nolan felt.

Nolan pulled Lacey back into his arms, unable to fight the temptation to stir the pot.

He needed something to take his mind off of Randi.

"We need to talk," Carter told Lacey as he approached.

And the look on Carter's face made Nolan positive that he'd be nice and distracted from Randi for the foreseeable hours.

Thank God.

CHAPTER
ONE

"OH, NOLAN'S HERE!" Annabelle waved at someone behind Randi.

Randi's heart thudded and she hunkered down over her margarita, taking a long pull on the straw.

And of course she and Annabelle were perched at a tall table in the middle of Bad Brews where he'd see them immediately even if Annabelle wasn't waving at him like he was a soldier returning from war.

Dammit.

It had been five months since she'd seen Nolan. And kissed him. And basically asked him to take her to bed.

And been turned down.

She'd known the sabbatical wouldn't last. Nolan came to Bad on a fairly regular basis from his big-shot city life in San Antonio. In fact, this absence had been longer than usual. According to the rumor mill, he'd been working on his book, had taken three trips to New York, and covered four huge stories for the newspaper that had all blown up into national stories. There were a couple of pretty crooked politicians in his neck of the woods.

Yeah, okay, so she'd read those. She followed the San Antonio
newspaper online specifically to read his stories. So what?

But she was glad he'd been busy. She'd loved every Nolan-
free/humiliation-free weekend since Coach's party.

"Oh, he's coming over," Annabelle said with a grin.

Of course he was.

Randi sucked harder on her straw.

"Hey, Annabelle."

His voice sounded deeper. Which was completely stupid. But
there was something about knowing what a great kisser he was
that made her attribute other things to him that she found hot.
Deep voices, big hands, nice asses. Those kinds of things.

"Hi, Nolan," Annabelle said. "You back for the weekend?"

"I'm back for a week or so, actually," he said. "Doing some
follow-up stuff for the book."

A week. Randi bit back a groan. She was going to have to
avoid him or act normal around him—and not like she was
dying of embarrassment over how she'd thrown herself at him—
for a week? That was going to be tough. Randi didn't get embarrassed. Until she was around Nolan Winters.

The stupid party hadn't been the first time. It seemed every
time they tried to have a one-on-one conversation, she ended up
feeling like an uneducated, silly, have-to-work-hard-for-a-C
student. Because that's always what she had been. But Nolan
was the only one that made her feel that way. It wasn't his fault.
He didn't do it on purpose. But she just wasn't able to hold her
own with a near-genius who was into politics and world events
and history.

If he'd wanted to talk transmissions and drag racing and
country music, she would have been fine. But he didn't.

This damned margarita was taking its time, Randi thought.
She could use a little buzz here.

"Hey, Randi."

In spite of everything, his voice made something low and

deep tighten inside of her. She lifted her head. She was polite, if nothing else. "Hey, Nolan."

"I think you owe me a dance."

She blinked at him. A dance. Because they hadn't danced at Coach's party. She'd been too busy putting her tongue down his throat and begging him to have sex with her. Basically.

"Sorry, I've probably had too much tequila."

The words were out before she really thought about them. But hey, *he* was the one who had decided she'd had too much of the cactus nectar the last time they'd been together. Still, Randi acknowledged that she had trouble controlling her sassiness sometimes. That sassiness had covered up many uncomfortable, self-conscious moments for her over the years and was definitely her fallback.

But instead of being offended, Nolan's mouth curled up into a smile. A sexy smile, if she was being honest.

"I kind of like it when you've had too much tequila."

So he did know what she was talking about. She lifted an eyebrow. "That's not how I remember it."

"Come dance and I'll remind you."

His hands had seemed big when they'd been on her ass. She remembered that part. And she loved big hands. And guys who would grip her hips or ass with those hands when they were making out. And when they were doing more than making out.

Dammit.

"I'm not really looking for a *dance* tonight," she said.

"What're you lookin' for?"

And there was a little hint of his Louisiana drawl. That had been distinctly missing from his words since he'd moved to San Antonio. Which was crazy. San Antonio was Texas and there was a drawl there. But Nolan had never had the deep accent a lot of the guys did in Bad, and he'd "cleaned up" since he'd gone to the city. He rarely wore jeans—Coach's party had definitely been an exception. He seemed to prefer dress slacks and button-down shirts, sometimes with a jacket, and he hadn't put a cap on his head in years.

According to all the gossip she heard, anyway. Though she had noticed his speech and dress on his visits to Bad too. And mourned the absence of denim. Blue jeans were *always* her preference, even over a tuxedo. Though the last time she'd seen one of those on a guy around here was prom, and it wasn't like those were the best look. The guys looked nervous and uncomfortable in the ill-fitted, hot, cumbersome things.

Annabelle kicked her under the table. Randi started and realized she'd been staring at Nolan as her thoughts turned. He was simply watching her, that grin in place, letting his question about what she was looking for hang in the air between them.

What was she looking for? A Bad boy. Who could make her heart hammer and her stomach flip. A Bad boy she wanted to dance with. Tequila or not.

"More tequila," she told him instead.

Because *he* was a Bad boy who made her heart hammer and her stomach flip. And she wanted to dance with him. But he wasn't really a *Bad* boy. Not anymore. He'd grown up here...but he'd grown beyond Bad. He wasn't a small-town kid anymore.

She was.

She always would be.

But for a moment she recognized the emotion in her throat. Wistfulness.

She loved Bad, and after twenty-eight years here, there wasn't much for surprises anymore.

That had to explain her strange and sudden reaction to Nolan. He was a surprise. Or the way he made her feel hot and tingly when she looked at his lips and remembered their kiss was a surprise, anyway.

"I need to ask you a question," he said. "Maybe I can buy you the next round, then and we can talk."

Talk? Hell no. That was the last thing she wanted to do with Nolan Winters. It was the only time she felt like a dumbass.

Other than the one time she'd tried to dry hump him in Coach's backyard.

The music on the jukebox changed to a Sam Hunt song she loved and she slid off the high chair. "On second thought, dancing sounds great."

Because what she couldn't add to a conversation about current events or politics, she could more than make up for on a bar dance floor. Typically the guys she hung out with wanted to talk about the same things she did—sports, cars, the locals—and when they ran out of words, they danced and drank. She could do all of those things 'til early in the morning.

Nolan didn't talk about sports or cars, and he didn't strike her as the gossipy type, so they were going to have to go straight to the dancing and drinking after all.

Good thing that, no matter how smart they were and how they dressed, all guys could be distracted by two things—boobs and compliments.

———

Randi was dressed up again tonight. It was February, so she was in jeans instead of a short summer dress, but she still wore her boots. And when she shrugged out of the jacket she was wearing, her fitted red top still clung to the most gorgeous pair of breasts he knew.

She grabbed his hand and tugged him toward the dance floor. Nolan was a smart guy—he followed without complaint.

This was swaying music, so he took her in his arms. He needed to gauge if she was right about the too-much-tequila tonight. He had a proposition and he wanted her honest answer. And he wouldn't mind picking up where they'd left off at Coach's, if she seemed so inclined.

He'd been thinking about her nonstop for the past five months. No, more than thinking about her. He'd been worked up about her. Previously, he'd always been able to put her out of his mind when he was away from Bad. Once in awhile he'd find himself comparing the city girls to her. It would start off as a compare and contrast between city girls and country girls in general, but when he was comparing caviar to buffalo wings, champagne to tequila and orchestra music to country twang, it didn't take long for his mind to go to Randi. But it wasn't like he obsessed about her all the time. He didn't even think about her every day.

But since Coach's party, he had been. And frankly, he was on edge tonight. He was trying not to show it, but the second he'd set foot in Bad this trip, he'd decided he was going to see what it was like to kiss a completely sober Randi.

She and that kiss were the whole reason for this trip.

The book was a great front. He could always talk to somebody here about football or Coach. And he did have a few chapters to go. He also needed to figure out photos. He had a photographer lined up for whenever he was ready, but he needed to figure out what he wanted in the book, and to best capture Coach and Bad and the love for the game that permeated the fabric of this town. But the book was just his cover for coming back to see Randi after finally getting his lips and hands on her.

He'd intended to get back here before this. If he hadn't had to wait five months, he might not be on the verge of throwing her over his shoulder and heading to her house right this minute. But he hadn't had a chance to get back. He'd been to New York three times and had been working on his book, as well as still doing all his writing for the *San Antonio Express-News*. There hadn't been any damned time. And now that he'd seen her, he was fighting to not pull her close, slide his hands under the back of her shirt onto hot, bare skin and lay a kiss on her unlike any she'd ever had.

But he wouldn't do it in public.

Partly because he hadn't yet determined how sober or drunk she was—though if she was too drunk again tonight, he was heading straight home for a cold shower and then a bottle of tequila of his own. He needed an outlet for this pent-up energy. He hadn't gotten rip-roaring drunk in too long. They said to write drunk and edit sober, but he'd never had a lot of luck with that approach. Between his book and the paper, he'd been far too sober for far too long.

And he wouldn't kiss Randi in public because he was afraid she'd push him back and demand to know what the hell he thought he was doing. In front of everyone. He wasn't fucking doing that. Even if he was twenty-eight and past all of those insecurities.

They didn't talk. Randi held herself stiffly in his arms and seemed to be lost in thought. But as Thomas Rhett switched to Carrie Underwood, Nolan felt her relax a little, and by the time Little Big Town came on, he felt enough tension leave her that he could pull her closer, and she came without a protest. When an old Garth Brooks floated out of the jukebox, she gave a big sigh, stepped completely up against Nolan and rested her head on his shoulder.

Suddenly he felt a lot of his own tightness flow out of him. He didn't need tequila or a cold swim or even hard-against-the-wall sex. He just needed her in his arms.

Damn. He was in trouble.

She felt good, she smelled good, and when she took her hand from his and wrapped both arms around his neck, Nolan felt a kick in his chest.

Two more songs played before she turned her head toward his face. Her lips were millimeters from his neck when she said, "I'm not drunk."

He swallowed, his skin feeling hot and a new tension filling his body. This was a whole lot less frustration and unrequited want and a lot more pure *need*.

"Glad to hear it." Really, really glad to hear it.

"The margarita on the table was my first and I didn't even finish it."

Nolan pulled back and looked down at her. "Say it." He had relaxed since getting here—since getting *her* up against him. But he wasn't going to play around and tease about this.

She lifted her head and looked him directly in the eye. "I want to kiss you again."

He studied her face. She was completely sincere. And sober.

Nolan pulled a long breath in through his nose. A breath full of the scent of peaches. That scent had always made him think of her. He didn't know if it was her shampoo or a body wash or what. But he intended to find out just how much of her smelled like peaches. "Not here," he said simply.

She nodded.

He took her hand and started for the door of the bar. He still needed to ask her for the favor he needed, but that could wait until after the kissing. Everything in the world could now wait until after the kissing.

Making out with Miranda Doyle in the bed of a pickup down by the bayou had been a long, longtime fantasy. Unfortunately, he no longer had a pickup.

She waved at Annabelle, who was watching them cross the bar with wide eyes and a knowing smile. Nolan didn't care who saw them leaving or what they thought about the reason.

He stopped by the door though. "You need to pay or give Annabelle a ride home or anything?" he asked Randi.

She reached around him and pushed the door open, nudging him through with her body. "I have a tab and Annabelle has a Jackson."

Her breasts pressed against his biceps, her feet tangled with his, and Nolan wrapped an arm around her waist to keep them from tumbling onto the stoop of Bad Brews.

"Easy, Ladybug," he said softly.

Randi got her feet under her and jerked upright. "What did you call me?"

He thought fast. Shit. He'd called her Ladybug. What the

fuck? They did *not* have a relationship that leant itself to nicknames.

But in ten years, he hadn't forgotten about that ladybug tattoo.

The door to Bad Brews shut behind them, leaving them alone in the suddenly quiet night.

"Nolan? Why did you call me Ladybug?" she asked.

He cleared his throat. "Your tattoo." What was the point in lying about it?

She lifted a brow. "You remember my tattoo?"

She really had no idea how much he knew and remembered about her. And to keep from freaking her out, he decided to downplay. "If it was on your ankle, I might have forgotten." There was no way in hell he would have forgotten. "But it was on your hip. Kinda low, if I remember right." He definitely remembered right. "You were wearing purple panties the night you showed me too."

There was a tiny smile tugging at the corner of her mouth. "You remember the color of my panties?"

He shrugged. "If they'd been white cotton and boring, probably not." He totally would have. "But they were purple silk. That stuck."

The tiny smile grew a little bigger. "They had a big white heart on the front."

Nolan felt a flash of heat go through him. From talking about a white heart on the panties that she'd worn ten years ago. Jesus, he was in huge trouble.

"I would have definitely remembered *that* if I'd seen it," he told her.

"If you would have seen that, I think you would have been remembering a lot of other things too," she said with a twinkle in her eyes and a smile that made everything male in Nolan go on high alert.

"How about we go make some memories now?" he asked.

He wasn't going to mess around here. This wasn't a one-night stand waiting to happen. He and Randi had known each other all their lives. There had never been any of this heat between them before, but it was there now. He was one of the smartest guys in Bad. He was getting Randi Doyle naked tonight.

"Sounds good." She stepped close and wrapped her arms around his neck. She put her lips to his ear and said huskily, "Know what I've been thinking about since you were here last?"

Nolan's hands were on her hips and he swore that if he didn't get his hand full of breast within the next three seconds, he was going to spontaneously combust. He slid a hand up her side until his thumb skimmed over the outer curve of one breast. "What?" he asked, his voice rough.

"The high school newspaper office."

The words took a second to sink in. "What about it?"

"I want to go there. With you."

He didn't move his hand, his thumb very happy resting against the fullness of her right breast, but he pulled back to look at her. "You want to go to the high school newspaper office? Now?"

She nodded, giving him a smile that should have been sweet, but was very naughty.

"Why?"

She lifted an eyebrow. "Really?"

"Yeah. Why there?"

There was light out here but the night shadows fell over them so that he couldn't tell for sure, but he thought she might be blushing.

"Forget it. It's stupid." She ducked her head. "We can go to my place."

She started to move back, but that would have taken her breast away from his thumb, so he gripped her hip with his other hand. "Hang on."

She looked up at him. "What?"

He turned them so the front light from Bad Brews shown on

her face. Then he reluctantly moved his hand from her side to her cheek, tipping her head slightly. Yep, she was blushing.

"What are you thinking about the newspaper office, Randi?" he asked.

"Nothing. It was a dumb idea. I didn't think."

Why did their conversations always have to be so damned weird?

Nolan swallowed his frustration and ran the pad of his thumb over her jaw. "I'd love to know. That newspaper office meant a lot to me in high school."

He'd been king there. He hadn't been an all-state football player—or anything player. He hadn't been Homecoming king or team captain or Mr. Popularity, but he'd been the editor of the school newspaper and the school's correspondent to the town newspaper. That meant he had something very important that the rest of them didn't, something more important than trophies, crowns and votes—he had control over information.

"I know it was," Randi finally said. "I shouldn't have suggested we have sex there."

Surprise and a major dose of lust rocked through him. "You were suggesting we go have sex there?"

Now the blush was easy to see even without direct lighting. "That's ridiculous, right?" she asked. "I know. I'm sorry. Maybe I did have more tequila than I thought."

She tried to duck her head again, but he cupped her face, forcing her to maintain eye contact. "You're not drunk."

She wet her lips and he almost groaned. He hadn't kissed her for months but he could still remember the exact feel and taste of her.

"Randi," he said. "You're not drunk." He wanted to hear it again.

"No."

"Then this isn't about tequila."

"It's..." She sighed heavily. "I say the stupidest things around you."

He supposed that he knew she was aware of the awkward-
ness when they talked one-on-one, but that was the first time
they'd really acknowledged it. "Things do get…"

He wasn't sure what word to use.

"Weird," she filled in.

He nodded and felt a smile forming. It was the best word.
"Yeah. Why do you think that is?"

She wrinkled her nose and focused on his cheek instead of
his eyes. "Me."

"You what?"

"It's because of me."

He frowned. "Our conversations get weird because of you?"

Her eyes came back to his. "Yeah."

"Why do you think that?"

She wet her lips again. "You know how when you're having
a normal conversation with someone, even if your mind really *is*
on what you're both saying, you have other thoughts going
through you mind too? Like if they have a button missing or if
it's hot in the room or that you only have five more minutes
before you need to leave…things like that?"

He nodded. He thought he was following. But just like she
said—his mind was on the conversation, but his thoughts
included things like the shape of her mouth and the fact that he
loved peaches and remembering the first time he'd seen her in
her cheerleading uniform.

"Well, since we have almost nothing in common, we run out
of normal conversation really fast, and then all that's left are all
those extra random thoughts. And I can keep them inside with
everyone else except you. I mean, I just *leave* other conversations
when I run out of things to say," she told him, clearly exasper-
ated. "But I can't leave you. And I can't keep all the stupidity
inside, apparently."

Nolan just watched her, processing that. He liked it. Yes, their
interactions were…memorable. But he liked that he affected her
differently than anyone else did. Her explanation about the

random thoughts in their heads made sense. He supposed he was surprised that showing him her tattoo and her peach-flavored body powder were two of her random thoughts when she talked to him.

"See?" she said. "Even this is weird. This is why I was hoping we'd stick with dancing and kissing."

"You turned me down for the dance," he said, still thinking about what she'd revealed.

"Yeah, until you wanted to talk."

He focused. "You pulled me on the dance floor to avoid talking?"

She nodded. "I like dancing with you."

"But not talking?"

"I feel like an idiot when we talk. Like right now."

He narrowed his eyes. "You don't need to feel like an idiot."

"Why not? I'm saying idiotic things."

"Do you want to see my tattoo and my body powder is peach flavored are not *idiotic*," he told her.

Her cheeks heated again and she stepped back until he had no choice but to let his hand drop.

"Dammit, Nolan. Do you remember every dumbass thing I ever said to you?"

He wouldn't categorize them as dumbass, but yeah, he probably did. "I have a really good memory. It's not you, it's me," he told her.

That got a tiny smile. "Well, that's definitely not true," she said. "But that's cute."

"Cute enough to go back to the newspaper office idea?" he asked. But he knew the moment was past. He tucked his hands into his pockets. *Fuck.*

"Sorry." She took a big breath and shrugged. "I can't explain it, Nolan," she said, her eyes full of a strange combination of confusion and frustration and maybe a touch of regret. "I get worked up around you and my mouth runs away with me—

either saying the dumbest stuff I've ever said to anyone or I'm kissing you like I'm some desperate, horny lush."

Something about all that made him step forward and take her upper arms in his hands. "You are not dumb and you're not desperate. And I don't care if we're talking or kissing—I *like* when your mouth runs away with you."

Then he sealed his lips over hers and kissed her with all the pent-up emotions he'd been carrying around since the last time.

It took only two seconds for her to moan and press closer. He moved his hands to her ass and her arms went around his neck. Their tongues stroked, their breathing grew ragged and their hands began wandering. Nolan walked her back until she was against the side of Bad Brews. His hand went back to the breast that he'd barely brushed earlier, now cupping it, reveling in how fucking perfect it felt, and playing with the hard tip through her shirt and bra. Randi made a soft, needy sound in her throat, and he nearly ripped her clothes off right then and there.

He tore his mouth away from hers. "The back door of the school still broken?"

She nodded. "You ever get a blowjob in that office?"

Nolan choked on the breath he'd been trying to take. He'd never gotten a blowjob within the Bad city limits. "You want to—"

The door to Bad Brews whacked Nolan in the back.

"Oh my God, I'm sorry!" Annabelle apologized as she walked through and let the door swing shut behind her.

Nolan slowly straightened away from Randi, taking his hand from her breast long before he was ready. Again.

Just then, Jackson came striding up the front walk. "What's up, everyone?"

It was a casual question but when Nolan turned, he saw Jackson's sharp gaze taking in every detail.

"I thought you guys had already left," Annabelle said.

"Yeah, we were…talking," Randi said.

Nolan glanced at her. She looked frustrated. He wasn't sure if it was the reminder of yet another strange one-on-one interaction with him or if it was their making out getting interrupted, but it made him want to pull her close and tell her it was okay.

"I love *talking*," Jackson said, his emphasis on the last word making it clear he knew they hadn't been only talking.

Annabelle peered at Randi. "You okay?"

Randi ran a hand through her hair. "I'm fine."

Nolan really hoped that wasn't true. Because *he* definitely wasn't fine.

"Need a ride?" Jackson asked Randi.

"Nope. Totally sober," she told him. "Really, really sober," she added on a mutter.

Nolan almost grinned at that.

"Okay, you ready to go?" Jackson asked his fiancée.

Anabelle shot Randi another look but nodded. "Yeah."

"You two," Jackson said, pointing at Nolan. "Be good."

Nolan sighed. Yeah. He had a feeling he was going to be good for the rest of the night. And alone. And horny.

———

"'Night, Nolan," Randi said, slipping around him. "I'll see you."

He reached out and snagged her wrist before she could escape. She groaned and turned to face him.

She just kept making an ass out of herself with him. She really wanted it to stop. Now. And the only way that seemed possible was if she just stayed away.

"I still have a question for you."

"But see, asking and answering questions will require talking. And we're not very good at that."

Okay, *she* wasn't very good at that. She was the one who sounded like an idiot. Why had she said that about the newspaper office? Just because it had occurred to her as kind of fun and naughty, didn't mean it wasn't totally stupid.

He smiled. "Maybe we just need more practice."

"More practice than the twenty-some years we've had?"

"It's not like we've had a lot of in-depth conversations in those twenty years," he reminded her.

She supposed that was true. She didn't remember starting to act crazy around him until about their junior year of high school. She'd always known him. She'd always liked him, for that matter. But either they hadn't had one-on-one conversations before their junior year or she hadn't been self-conscious about them until then, for whatever reason.

Randi remembered the first time she'd shoved her foot in her mouth. They'd been at a party at Carter's dad's house, their junior year, football season. They'd ended up by the stereo together, alone. They'd said awkward hi's and then she'd said something about the football game. That topic lasted about three seconds. Nolan covered the games for the paper but she knew he didn't really *care*. Not like she did. She'd loved football her entire life and could go on and on about it. With anyone else in the room, that would have been fine, great even. A lot of the guys thought her love and knowledge of the game was sexy. But she knew Nolan didn't want to talk about the game. So she'd clenched her teeth together and told herself to just shut up. To fill the stupid silence, he had said something about geometry. Geometry was a horrible class. She hated it and it was tough for her. She had been barely pulling her C at that point. But she didn't want Nolan to know that she wasn't very smart. So she'd tried to distract him. Or something. She still wasn't sure *why* she'd asked if he wanted to see her tattoo. But it had worked to stop the conversation train that was barreling toward a massive wreck.

"I think I'd rather kiss you than talk to you," she said honestly. "No offense."

He gave a rough laugh. "I don't think I'm offended. Though I'm not sure."

She felt a little smile quirk. "Are you sure you don't just want to come over to my house?"

He looked at her for a long moment, studying her face, searching her eyes—and suddenly Randi knew exactly why she was so awkward around him, scrambling to cover her lack of knowledge about anything outside of Bad, Louisiana.

He saw her.

When he looked at her, it wasn't the way the other guys did. Men looked at her—always had—and saw her boobs and butt and mouth and hair and whatever else it was that guys liked. She'd been told those specific things were "sexy as hell" and made her "completely fuckable" several times in her life.

But Nolan didn't see those things. Or not *only* those things. He looked beyond all of that. And that freaked her out. Because she wasn't sure how much else was really there. She was a hell of a mechanic. She was kind, generous, fun, a good friend and daughter and sister. She was proud of all of that and she was content with her life in Bad. But for some reason, she felt as if being content with small-town life, the same faces and places every day, somehow made her less in some people's eyes. Like Nolan's.

It was no secret that he'd been eager to leave Bad and that he loved life in San Antonio. Sure, he came back to visit and seemed happy to see everyone and hang out for a few days here and there. But his job for the newspaper required travel all over the country, and since he'd written that first book, he was going to New York every so often. He'd outgrown Bad—while she'd barely grown at all.

That was how it felt, anyway.

"No, I don't think I'm coming over tonight," Nolan finally said, letting go of her wrist. "But I *am* going to ask my question."

Oh, boy. "Fine. What?"

"Will you help me with my book?"

"Your book?" she repeated. "The one you're writing about Coach?"

"Yes."

"You want to interview me or something?" She loved Coach.

She had some great stories.

"Yes," he said. "But more. I need a football expert to be sure I'm getting game details and terminology right."

She blinked at him. She knew football. Every nuance and detail. But a hundred other people—probably more—right here in Bad knew as much as she did. Well, almost as much as she did. "Why me?"

"You know everything about the program, the history, the players, the town."

"So do lots of other people."

"I want to see if we can have a normal conversation," he said. "I'm giving us a common topic."

Randi narrowed her eyes. "That's the only reason?"

"No, I really need the help. You know what I need to know. And you smell better than the other people I could ask."

She felt herself smile at that. "What kind of questions?"

He shrugged. "Is there any football question I could ask that you *wouldn't* know the answer to? Honestly?"

She had to admit that having free reign to go on and on about football sounded pretty great. And the idea of talking with authority about something to *Nolan* was really tempting. She'd love to show off a little—or a lot—after all the times she'd made a fool of herself.

"Okay, I can help."

His face relaxed into a big grin immediately. "Awesome. Thanks."

"Sure. How do you want to do this?"

"How about I come to the shop tomorrow?" he asked. "We can chat while you work? Or will that be distracting?"

Her optimism about the deal increased significantly with that. "Yes, the shop would be great." With a wrench in her hand and the smell of motor oil surrounding her, she'd be as at ease as much as she possibly could. Work would distract her from feeling self-conscious around him. It was the perfect setup. "I get there at six."

"I'll be there at six o'one."

They'd have the shop to themselves until seven thirty when Luke came in. That could be good. Easier to talk. Or bad. Because it would be easier to talk.

"I'll see you then." She started to turn to finally make her escape.

"Randi."

She stopped and glanced back.

"Sorry about the Ladybug thing. That was out of line."

She stared at him for a moment. She wasn't sure she'd ever had a guy apologize for being out of line with her. Voluntarily, anyway. She'd gotten an apology after bloodying a guy's nose in fifth grade. She'd gotten one after kneeing a guy in the balls in ninth grade. And she'd gotten one after she'd taken a guy's transmission apart, in the parking lot of the baseball field while he was playing third base, the summer after they graduated.

But she couldn't remember a time when someone just offered one.

And it figured that he was apologizing for something that didn't bother her at all. He'd surprised her with it. As had the thump her heart made after he'd said it. "You don't have to apologize for that," she told him honestly.

"That was kind of...personal of me, though," he said.

She nodded. "But I don't mind you being personal with me." And she meant it. He made her feel awkward and jittery and reminded her that she wasn't the brightest bulb in the drawer, but he had never said or done anything to make her think that *he* thought that. She was just a little overwhelmed by how smart he was and how sophisticated he'd become. And that was on her, not him.

Then she turned and headed for her car, before her mouth started running again and she said something like "how do you feel about dirty talk in bed?" or "I don't suppose you're a hair-puller?"

CHAPTER
TWO

RANDI LOOKED HOT AS HELL.

Nolan had to actually adjust himself as he approached the huge open door of the shop. She was in jeans, a white tank top, her dark hair piled up under a ball cap. She was up on a wooden block, bent over under the hood of a truck, and he wanted nothing more than to run his hands over the sweet curve of her ass.

A woman in an evening gown and heels had never affected him that much.

Instead, he cleared his throat.

She looked up with a smile. "Morning."

"Morning." He held out a cup of coffee.

She took it. "Wow, what a gentleman."

He knew that there was coffee here at the shop, but he had spent almost five minutes staring at the donuts, not knowing what to bring her. He didn't even know if she liked donuts, not to mention what kind. Why he felt the need to bring her something, he couldn't really say, but he'd finally just poured two cups of coffee.

Which now seemed pretty stupid. He'd had his car worked on down here before. The things that could be counted on at the auto shop were excellent service, dirty jokes, swearing loudly, and hot, strong coffee. The best part—and Nolan wasn't the only one who thought so—the funniest, dirty jokes and the loudest swearing usually came from Randi.

He dug in his pocket and pulled out several packets of sugar, a few of low-cal sweetener, and five tiny tubs of creamer, both plain and hazelnut.

He had no idea how Randi took her coffee.

Of course, as he dumped the cream and sugars on the edge of the truck she was working on, he realized that since she did work here—owned the place, in fact—she probably had whatever cream and sweetener she needed too.

He looked up to find her grinning at him. "Thanks."

"I wanted to cover the bases."

She nodded. "Done."

He felt like an idiot.

Why did one of them always feel stupid around the other?

He sighed. This was not going to continue. He could just drop the whole thing. He could just consider Randi a friend from high school. They could keep socializing in groups and having the occasional awkward conversation…where he sometimes got to see her bare hip. That hadn't been all bad.

But he wanted to take her to New York with him. He had a huge party coming up with his publisher and he needed a date. He hadn't been able to even consider anyone else since Randi had kissed him at Coach's party. But if they couldn't get through ten minutes without being awkward and something strange happening, it would be a no-go.

But if they *could* have a normal one-on-one interaction, then it was a green light. There wasn't another woman he wanted to take. He'd considered asking his friend Bailey to go, just so he wasn't dateless, or stuck with a blind date set up by his agent's assistant, or trapped for a weekend in New York with one of the women he'd dated here and there in San Antonio. He'd done all of the above and none appealed at all.

Especially when there was even the slightest chance that he could take Randi.

Far from Bad, in the bright lights and big city, just the two of them, for a whole weekend. Sounded like paradise to him.

Of course he knew it would be out of her comfort zone. But he simply couldn't imaging taking someone else. And he wanted to give her some Cinderella treatment. He wanted to buy her a fancy dress and some sparkly jewelry and give her an afternoon at the spa and, yeah, he wanted to show her the big city, and hold her hand and dance with her. And take her back to a fancy hotel suite and…

Yeah. He wanted to sweep her off her feet and impress her.

"You okay?" she asked.

"Yes." He absolutely was. This was going to be great. They were going to have a great time here over the next couple of days, and he was going to convince her to fly to New York with him in two weeks.

"So how do you want to do this?"

He held up his notebook. "I'll just ask questions as you work?"

"Great. You can sit right there." She pointed to an overturned plastic bucket. But she dropped her arm a moment later. "No, hang on."

She headed into the office and started to pull a chair into the garage. The bottom of the chair caught on the doorway and she fought with it for a moment.

"Randi, no, this is good. I'm fine." He started for the bucket. If that's what people sat on around here… Then again, people probably didn't sit around out here much. This was the work area. The clients sat in the waiting room with the coffee pot and the TV that was perpetually turned to ESPN.

"You'll get dirty sitting on that." She gave the chair a hard yank and it came loose, causing her to stumble slightly and swear as the back of her hand banged against the doorframe.

GOT IT BAD · 39

"Dammit, Randi, I'm fine." He crossed to her and took the chair from her, then lifted her hand.

She watched as he ran his thumb over the back where she'd whacked it.

He pressed a kiss to the spot.

"Nolan?" she said softly.

"Yeah?"

"I get bruises and cuts and scrapes every day. My job is kind of manual and hands-on."

Just another huge difference between them. He sat at a computer in an office and wrote for a living. She got her hands, and the rest of her, dirty and greasy and yeah, probably even a little bloody. Damn.

"But it's a great excuse to kiss you," he said, kissing the spot once more.

She took a big breath, but then her fingers curled around his. "You don't need to make up excuses."

He stepped closer.

But she put her other hand up. "I'll get you dirty."

"I hope so." Then he wrapped an arm around her waist and hauled her up against him, kissing her.

She melted into him a lot faster than she had on the dance floor. He liked that.

He knocked her cap off, tunneled his fingers into her hair, and opened his mouth, drinking her in, tasting her thoroughly.

She gave in. For a little bit. She not only let him taste her, but she tasted him back.

But long before Nolan was ready to let her go, he felt her hands against his chest, pushing.

He let her step back. For now.

"I have to work," she said. Her voice was husky.

"Me too."

"Then you need to sit down. And I need to get back under that hood."

"You've never looked sexier than when you're under that hood."

She smiled and lifted a hand. She rubbed her thumb over his jaw. "I got you dirty."

"We're just getting started."

He saw how her breath caught at his words, but she moved back, picked up her cap, tucked her hair back underneath it, and went over to the car.

"You can put the chair wherever you want in here."

Okay, time to work. He should sit on the chair. It was right there. It would be much more comfortable. But something told him that he needed to sit on the bucket. She was worried about getting him dirty, but he knew there was more to it. There was something there, something deeper. He couldn't put his finger on it exactly, and he didn't have time to delve into it now. But he would. He had a very good memory.

———

She'd never had this much trouble concentrating on her work before. She was pretty sure the fifteen-year-old truck that Henry Choate, had hauled in here was going to be in her shop for a few days. She was going to need to order a part. Or two. But she wanted to recheck everything. Nolan was distracting her to the point that she hated to tell the guy he was stranded in town and out a few hundred bucks for her to order something when really it was just a corroded battery or something.

This was crazy. But she couldn't deny that she loved having Nolan there. The work was taking twice as long as it should, but she liked the feeling of his eyes on her and the sound of his voice.

And they were having a conversation without her acting like a crazy person. Of course, they were talking about football. In her auto shop. This was her comfort zone. She was happy here, and more, she was confident here. And that was a lot of why she liked having Nolan around. She liked him, but she needed that boost of confidence. At least if they were going to do more than kiss. Because she was a great kisser.

"Okay, so third quarter. They were down by a touchdown. Why did Coach go for two instead of pushing for a touchdown?"

She grinned and launched into an explanation about the strategy of play-calling in the third quarter of a football game. Nolan was taking notes and she took a moment to appreciate talking to a man about football who didn't feel the need to correct her and input his own opinions every other word.

She didn't mind opinions, when they were well-formed, but she *did* mind being corrected. She knew two things better than anyone in this town and *no one* corrected her on football or cars. Not without regretting it, anyway.

"Why do you love this game so much?"

She looked up. He was watching her with true interest. That wasn't about football. That was about her.

But she wanted to answer. "My grandpa."

"He taught you about the game?"

She nodded and moved to the other side of the car so her back, or rather her butt, was to him. Maybe if she didn't look at him while she told him personal things, she wouldn't sound silly. "When I was little, he went to all of the Renegade football games and he took me with him. I'd sit on his lap and eat popcorn and drink soda—the only time I got soda—and I'd just cheer along whenever he did. I also learned to cuss at refs from him." She looked over her shoulder to shoot him a grin.

He was grinning back. And not looking at her ass. She straightened in surprise. She hadn't realized that she'd been expecting him to be looking at her ass. But guys always looked at her ass when they were in the shop and she was working.

She appreciated that Nolan wasn't, more than she would have thought.

Ironic, considering he was one guy she wouldn't mind looking his fill.

Randi propped a hip against the car and wiped her hands on the rag she kept tucked in her back pocket. "As I got older, I started watching it with him on TV too. Part of it was that I was starting to understand more about the game. Part of it was that it was the only time I could get away with swearing. I could cuss and yell things that, any other time, would have gotten my mouth washed out with soap, but during a football game, Mom and Grandma just ignored it. Plus, I learned to love chicken wings and nachos and beer."

"You got to drink beer during football games as a kid?" Nolan interrupted.

She laughed. "I got a sip of Grandpa's beer at the start of each quarter. It probably ended up being a mouthful total. But I thought I was really getting away with something."

"You had a wild streak even then."

She shrugged. She wasn't sure she'd been *wild*, but she definitely liked the thrill of breaking a rule here and there. "Anyway, I kept going to games with him until I was about ten. I even pulled his oxygen for him. But then he got really sick with the COPD and couldn't walk that far or climb the bleachers, so I would go to the games and call him, and we'd stay on the phone for the whole game, with me giving him the play-by-play. He also wanted me to fill in the downtime during timeouts and half-time with a game analysis. So I had to know what I was talking about."

"How'd you do that while you were cheering?" Nolan asked.

Randi felt her heart clench. "He died the summer before our sophomore year."

"I'm sorry, Randi."

For a split second, she wished that he'd called her Ladybug again. It was a silly little nickname that didn't even fit her, but when he'd called her that, she'd almost melted into a puddle.

She'd never almost melted into a puddle for a guy before. Ever.

"I miss him like crazy," she said with a nod. "Football became a way of feeling close to him after that. And by then, I was hooked. Hard."

Nolan looked like he wanted to say something else. Or maybe hug her. She really wanted him to hug her. But instead he asked, "So there's more to your obsession than your grandpa?"

"Oh, for sure."

"Explain that to me."

She pulled in a breath and turned back to the car. But she was able to move around to the other side, not feeling like she needed her back to him now.

"I love how physically tough it is. To be a star, you have to be strong, flexible, have amazing reflexes. But there's a ton of mental toughness needed too. You get banged up but you have to stay in there. And then there's the trash talk." She shot him another grin. "It's just such a *guy* thing."

She watched as Nolan's eyebrows went up and for a second she grimaced. Oops.

"That's not to say that a guy has to play football for me to like him."

Then she winced. That sounded just as bad.

"I mean, I love football players, but that's not the only way to be manly."

Nolan just kept watching her.

"I like muscles and stuff, but I don't *need* muscles." She was aware that her mouth was running away with her again. "That's not to say that *you* don't have muscles."

She pressed her lips together. *Shut up, Randi.*

He finally spoke. "Do you like me?"

Randi took a breath. "Yes."

"Good."

He didn't say anything else.

"I like big muscles, but not *just* big muscles." She needed to stop talking. She was aware of that. Still she went ahead and said, "I like brains too."

Nolan's mouth curved. "Good."

"I like your muscles too," she finished weakly. He wasn't linebacker huge but he was in great shape and when he wore T-shirts and jeans, it really showed.

"Thanks."

She waited, but he didn't say anything else. And she knew she needed to stop saying things. She crossed her arms and watched him back.

Nolan Winters could give any guy in Bad a run for his money. The slacks and polo he wore today didn't get her heart pounding the way worn denim did, but it didn't matter. She couldn't look at him without remembering the surprisingly hot and awesome things he could do with his mouth on hers. And wonder what it would be like to have that mouth on other places.

"I'm sorry," she finally said.

"For liking me and my brains and my muscles?" he asked, with clear amusement.

"For not being better at having conversations with you and for insinuating that you're not my type."

"Were you insinuating that?" he asked.

"Not intentionally. I just didn't want you to take that from what I said."

Nolan got up from the bucket and crossed to where she stood.

Randi instinctively straightened and dropped her arms.

He looked down at her. "You like me."

Definitely. He might intimidate her a little, and she might wish she was a little more worldly when he was around, but the answer was a definite, "Yes."

"That's all I need to know," he said.

"Really?"

"Yes." He paused. "Come to New York with me."

"What?"

"I have a big party in New York to attend in a couple of weeks. I need a date. I'd love to take you."

"Me?" Randi knew her eyes were wide. But a party in New York City? Randi had never been farther from home than San Antonio. And that had been to watch a football game. The traffic had boggled her mind.

And he was talking about New York City.

"Yes, you," Nolan said with a smile.

"I...don't know anything about New York. Or big, fancy parties."

"I'd love to show you."

There was something in his voice that made her look up into his eyes. She couldn't put her finger on it, but Nolan seemed very serious suddenly. But there was also a touch of something else...eagerness? Affection?

"I don't even know what to wear."

He nodded. "That's okay. We'll go a day early and I'll take you shopping."

Shopping in New York City? Randi had to admit that sounded fun. She'd just been thinking that Bad didn't have much for excitement. This would be an adventure.

"How much should I bring?" she asked, her thoughts spinning.

"Clothes? Very little."

Her eyes flew up to his. "What?" She felt a grin stretching.

"You won't need much. We'll get what you need there."

But a smile teased his lips, and she knew the double meaning she'd assumed behind his answer was accurate.

"I thought maybe you meant that, other than the party, we'd spend a lot of time in the hotel room so I wouldn't need a lot of outfits."

"Well, I thought I wanted to show you the city."

"But now?"

"Now I'm thinking about how fun hotel rooms can be."

So it might be that kind of trip. She had to admit that the Statue of Liberty didn't sound like the biggest draw to New York City suddenly.

"I'll have to take your word for it," she said. "I haven't ever been to New York and I haven't spent that many nights in hotel rooms."

Her family hadn't had the money to travel more than a road trip here and there in Louisiana. And, honestly, Randi had never been bitten by the travel bug. She knew there were some amazing places that she'd probably love seeing, but she also knew that there was very little in the world that could compare to the beauty of looking out at the view from her front porch. For her. She understood that wasn't true for everyone. But she was content. Mostly. Her life was pretty much what she'd always expected it to be. And she counted her blessings. She had a good life. Quiet, simple, surrounded by people she loved, doing things she loved.

If she wondered once in a while if there was more or if she was missing something, she figured that was normal.

"New York is amazing. And hotel rooms can be amazing," Nolan told her.

"Can be?" she asked.

"Depends on why you're there."

"You mean like they're fun when you're there for a big, fancy party?" she teased.

"With a gorgeous woman whose kisses have been keeping me up at night."

He didn't smile when he said that. He was completely serious. Randi felt herself swallowing hard. "Oh."

He seemed to realize he was being a little intense, because he leaned back. "But I really just want to treat you to a fun weekend in the city. You'll have your own room."

She felt a twinge of disappointment. But instead of commenting on it, she said, "Why do you want to treat *me*?"

"I love New York and you've never been. I thought it would be fun to show someone the city for the first time. Everyone I've been there with has been before."

Randi bit her tongue on asking if "everyone" meant women.

It did. It had to. She focused on how sweet it was that he wanted to show *her* the city. "That's really nice. If you want me to go with you, I'd love to."

"I want you to go with me."

"Okay."

The smile he gave her made her heart thump in a way she hadn't felt in a really long time. He looked like she'd just announced he'd been elected president. Wow, she hadn't made someone else feel like that in a really, really long time.

"I'm going to head home and work on this chapter," he said. "Maybe later you could come over and read through it for me? I want to be sure I got the game right."

The chapter was about the district championship game that had put the Renegades into the state playoffs. The playoffs that they'd ended up dominating. The crown jewel to their biggest and best season ever.

"That would be great," she agreed, realizing that she'd been expecting him to kiss her. And that she was disappointed that he hadn't. "Or you could come to my place. I'll make you dinner."

"Great plan," he agreed easily.

She wasn't a fantastic cook, but she wouldn't embarrass herself. At least, not with the food. Why did she keep agreeing to spend time with Nolan when she tripped over her words and ended up feeling like a jerk?

Because *he* seemed to want to keep spending time with *her*. In spite of all of that.

"How's seven?" she asked.

"I'll be there."

"Great."

"Should I bring the tequila?"

She tipped her head. She was still surprised by Nolan's teasing side. "I have plenty of tequila."

He gave her a grin. "Right. It was the shot glasses you didn't have."

Randi felt her stomach flip and she crossed her arms, trying to not show how easily he affected her. "Right."

"Have you gotten any since Coach's party?" Nolan asked.

"Nope. I just drink straight from the bottle."

He gave a nod. "That works. And I can use your belly button. So we should be good."

She was pretty sure he realized how that affected her because she blew out a quick breath and said, "Okay then, I'll be sure to wear something we can pull up."

He gave her a hot look. "Yeah. You do that."

Then he turned and walked away. Without kissing her. And she was still disappointed by it.

———

"Are you dating Miranda Doyle?"

Nolan looked up from his computer screen as his mother came in the back door of the house into the kitchen.

"Um."

"Are you dating Miranda Doyle?" Teresa Winters set her reusable grocery bag on the countertop, the canned goods making a loud thunk.

Nolan saved his work and leaned back in his chair. "Do not tell your Bunko ladies or the beauty shop girls that Randi and I are dating," he said. "That's very premature."

Teresa crossed her arms and leaned back against the counter. "So you want to."

"Where did you hear this?"

"Nicole told Janice that Kristine took her car into the shop this morning and you were there. With Miranda."

Nolan nodded. "That's true. She's helping me with this chapter."

Teresa gave him a look that said "don't bullshit me". "And then, as we were talking, Sandra said that Chad told her that you were dancing with her at Bad Brews."

Nolan sighed. One more thing he didn't miss about Bad. The freaking grapevine here was impressive—and scary.

"I danced with her. And I talked to her about football today. How does that add up to dating?" he asked. Of course, he did want to date Randi, but he knew how this conversation was going to go. His mother was nothing if not predictable. She'd always been very consistent on three things—Nolan was amazing, Nolan was nothing like his father, and Nolan was too good for Bad.

No one was more Bad than Miranda Doyle.

"Nolan Phillip Winters, you stay away from that girl."

Yep, this was exactly how this was going to go. "You said yourself that you would never trust anyone else with your car."

"She's a wonderful mechanic. She's a sweet girl. But she's not the right girl for you."

"Because she's from here?"

"Because she's from here and she's got no ambitions *beyond* here."

Exactly like Teresa. It was no deep dark secret to Nolan that his mother resented everything about Bad because she was stuck here. Or thought she was. And she blamed his father for it. She'd wanted to leave, to see the world. But she'd fallen for Nolan's father and gotten pregnant. She'd been happy. For a long time. She'd chosen love and she'd truly felt that was the right, ultimately rewarding thing to do.

Then his father had left her. And not just for another woman. He'd gone and traveled and done all of the things Teresa had wanted to do. The things that getting married and tied down with two kids and two jobs had kept her from doing.

Nolan had offered to bring her to San Antonio with him. But she couldn't easily leave now. Nolan's sister lived in Bad and had two kids Teresa adored. Teresa had a job that she actually liked, but no degree, no real option for doing anything else. And she owned her house. Nolan's father had sent her enough guilt money to pay off the mortgage. She couldn't live anywhere else as cheaply, and she'd never leave her grandkids. No matter how much Teresa had tried to encourage both of her kids to leave, to do more, to want more, her daughter Carly had followed right in her footsteps.

Carly getting pregnant with her first son at age sixteen had only increased Teresa's pressure on Nolan to get the hell out of Bad.

"I like Randi, Mom," Nolan said firmly. "If I want to see her while I'm here, I will."

"While you're here," Teresa said quickly, pointing her finger at him. "Fine. While you're here, do whatever you want. Just be sure you *leave* again. And *don't* knock her up."

Nolan blew out a breath. "Mom."

"Nolan."

"*Mom.*"

"Nolan, you got out. You did something with yourself. I'm *so* proud of you." Teresa crossed to his chair. She took his face in her hands. "You deserve everything you've got. Don't backtrack now for a girl."

"Mom, I am not backtracking by dating Randi. She's wonderful."

"And there are *thousands* of wonderful girls in San Antonio. Even more in New York."

Nolan decided that he needed to nip this in the bud.

He hadn't dated anyone seriously in high school, in part because his mother always started in on this shit after date three. And he hadn't ever cared about anyone enough to really fight with her about it. He'd always planned to leave Bad. Sure, it might have been in part because his mother had started the mantra about him being destined for greater things when he was about five. But he'd wanted to be a journalist since he was twelve, and he'd known he wanted to do more exciting stories than the winner of Tuesday night Bingo and the fender-benders on Main and the monthly anniversaries.

The Bad News, and the news it covered, was all very nice. Lost dogs and lawnmowers for sales, the menu for the senior center and the school, church service schedules, heartfelt obituaries and happy birth announcements. And, of course, the sports page. It was sweet. It was something he loved about Bad. But it wasn't what he wanted to do.

So leaving Bad hadn't been a difficult decision at all. After his mother had pounded the use of abstinence and condoms and double condoms into his brain, not getting seriously involved with a woman in Bad hadn't been a difficult decision either. He'd been ready to see the world, have some fun, hang out with a sophisticated crowd.

But now he was twenty-eight years old, very successful, living in San Antonio and traveling the country, and if he wanted to date the town's mechanic, he would.

"Mom, I'm taking Randi to a party in New York in two weeks."

Teresa gave him a look he'd seen directed at his sister a million times. It said "I can't believe how stupid you are".

"Nolan—"

He pushed his chair back and stood. "Mom, this isn't up for discussion. It's a party. In New York. I'm not putting a down payment down on a house in Bad. I'm not turning in my resignation. I'm not screwing up my future or flushing my options or potential or anything else down the toilet. I'm taking a woman I like to a party."

"A party in New York."

"Yes."

"With your publishing people."

Nolan smiled. "Yes."

"Do you really think that's a good idea?"

He nodded. "I do, actually."

"What is Miranda Doyle going to talk to a bunch of fancy New Yorkers about?" Teresa asked. "All that girl knows is cars, football and beer."

Nolan took his mother's upper arms, pulled her close and

kissed her forehead. "I happen to know they all drive cars, have heard of football and have tried beer."

Teresa did not look reassured. Nolan closed his computer and gathered his notes.

"Where are you going now?"

"To shower for my dinner date at Randi's."

He heard his mother's very heavy sigh as he headed toward the stairs.

"Well, do me one favor at least," she called after him.

He knew what was coming. "What's that?"

"Double condom."

Nolan paused on the bottom step. "I'll take six or eight. Just in case," he shot back.

Then he loped up the stairs, grinning, as his mother yelled, "That's not funny!"

———

Randi added a lime to her basket and started to turn away. Then grabbed another before continuing down the produce aisle. She had tequila and salt but she'd hate to run out of limes tonight.

She felt a little warmer just thinking about Nolan's lips closing around the lime where it rested—

She turned right at the end of the aisle, and ran directly into Bailey Davis.

"Oh, sorry!"

Bailey grinned at her. "What are you making him?"

For one second, Randi was surprised. Then she sighed. "Where did you hear?"

"Rhonda told Donna at the post office."

"Are you stalking me?" Randi asked.

"Do you mean, did I stop by the grocery store for carrots I didn't need because I heard you were making Nolan dinner? Yes."

Randi accepted the inevitable. Everyone in Bad knew she was

making dinner for Nolan tonight. They probably knew about the party in New York. There was no sense in playing dumb.

"Steak," she said in answer to Bailey's first question.

"Good call."

Yeah well, steak, burgers and anything else that went on the grill were her go-to's. She was an okay cook in the kitchen, but she was pretty great on the grill.

And steak went with tequila. Probably.

"Do you know if he likes dessert?" Randi asked. Bailey knew Nolan well. They'd gone to college in New Orleans together with Sabrina, Brooke, Luke, and Marc and had all hung out. Nolan had actually invited Bailey to be his plus one at an ex's wedding, but had gotten food poisoning and Luke had ended up taking Bailey and they'd crashed the wedding...and fallen in love.

"He likes dessert," Bailey confirmed. "But the basics—pie, cookies, brownies. I wouldn't worry about getting fancy."

Randi almost slumped in relief. She'd looked up some recipes for things like tortes and tiramisu but she'd been nervous about getting them right. Not that she really knew what went into making a torte. Or even what a torte actually was.

"Brownies? Really?" Pie was a little beyond her skill level too, but cookies and brownies she could do. Even from scratch.

Bailey nodded. "He likes stuff like meatloaf and spaghetti and roast chicken—normal, home-cooked type stuff."

Well, Randi could do all of those. She was feeling better and better all the time.

"How about appetizers? Do you think I should do something there?" Appetizers around here were chicken wings and mozzarella sticks, and if you ordered both you didn't have to worry about ordering a meal. Was the same true in New York and San Antonio?

Bailey gave her a smile. "No, I wouldn't worry about it. Steak, baked potato, green beans, brownies. You're set."

Randi looked at the other woman, fighting the urge to hug

her in the middle of the grocery store. "Really? I don't even need to do fancy potatoes?"

Bailey tipped her head. "What are fancy potatoes?"

Randi dug her phone out of her back pocket and swiped her thumb across the screen, pulling up the recipe for roasted red potatoes with parsley. She'd never used parsley in her life.

Bailey shook her head with a smile. "No. Bake them. You're fine."

"Thank God."

Bailey put a hand on her arm and gave her a gentle squeeze. "Thank you."

Randi frowned as she slid her phone back into her pocket. "What do you mean?"

"For asking him to dinner. He's such a great guy and I know that everyone here thought of him as kind of a nerd in high school. But he's just so…great," she finished, as if that was the best word she could come up with. "Thanks for giving him a chance."

Whoa. Randi shook her head. "I'm not giving him a chance." She sighed. "That's not what I meant. There's no chance." She shook her head again. "There's no reason I *wouldn't* give him a chance."

Dammit. She couldn't even talk *about* him without sounding stupid?

"What I mean," she said slowly, "is that I like Nolan. This is not some big favor or chance I'm taking here. I want to see him tonight and I'm really glad he's coming over."

Bailey smiled. "Well, he really likes you too."

"He told you that?" Obviously there was some chemistry between them and he'd asked her to the New York party. So yeah, she figured he liked her. But did he *like* her?

And since when had they all gone back to seventh grade?

"A long time ago," Bailey confirmed. "You're the one he always wanted a shot with but never got."

Randi shook her head. That definitely wasn't right. "You've got the wrong girl."

"No, it's you."

"No, I was…not his type." There hadn't been any spark between them in high school that she could recall. There had been no flirting, no hot looks, no mention of body shots.

She hadn't actually known about body shots in high school. Probably. She couldn't remember when she'd learned about body shots, to be honest. But she hadn't done them in high school. She'd done other stuff though. Plenty of it. And now that she thought about it, those were the things that made her less Nolan's type than the school-and-grades thing. She'd drunk beer and made out and snuck into places she wasn't supposed to be and snuck *out* of places she *was* supposed to be. Nolan had studied and tutored other people. While she'd been staying out late partying, he'd been staying up late reading. While she'd been taking road trips to see live bands, he'd been taking road trips to science camp.

She hadn't been his type because she hadn't taken anything seriously. While he'd taken everything seriously.

Except football. There they'd switched roles. Blitzes and option plays had been serious stuff to her. Nolan didn't know a fumble from a formation.

Bailey looked puzzled. "You don't think so?"

"No way."

"You're sweet, funny, talented, beautiful. What was his type?"

Not turned on by motors and transmissions. Not neck deep in football from August to January. Not pulling a C in history class.

Nolan had known everything there was to know about World War II, the sixties, the Reagan years, countries she'd never heard of, political theories that made her yawn.

He'd filled in for their history teacher for a week when he had gallbladder surgery and they couldn't get a sub. Nolan had covered Hitler's rise to power pre-World War II and, interestingly, those were the only things Randi still remembered now from nine months of American history fourteen years ago.

"We just had nothing in common," Randi finally answered Bailey. "I was taking motors apart while he was working on math extra credit. I took shop class. He took advanced-placement English."

Bailey smiled. "Well, I'm glad you found something in common now," she said. "Really. I know you'll have a great time tonight."

"Thanks."

Randi watched Bailey move off to pick out cantaloupes. Then she headed to the meat counter. And tried to tell herself they did indeed have something in common now. And that a book about Coach Karr and a love for tequila body shots was enough to keep them both interested for one night.

What they were going to do in New York, she had no idea. But one concentrated effort to not come off as an uncultured, small-town Louisiana tomboy at a time.

CHAPTER
THREE

STEAK, baked potatoes, green beans and brownies.

He was in heaven.

Add in a beautiful girl in a short skirt who smelled like peaches, and it was heaven in heaven.

"Did your mom teach you to cook?" he asked. Randi's mom was a nurse and her dad was an over-the-road trucker, home only two or three nights a week.

She nodded. "She tried. I frustrated the hell out of her, though."

He took a bite of the steak she'd grilled and gave a little groan. He looked over to see her watching him with a surprised but pleased look.

"It's good?"

"It's really good." He chewed and swallowed. "Why did teaching you to cook frustrate the hell out of her?"

"Because I thought it was a waste of time."

"How so?" He took another huge bite.

"You spend an hour, sometimes more, doing it and then it's over in like fifteen minutes," she said. "Drove me crazy."

"You spend hours fixing cars," Nolan pointed out.

"Yeah, but in the end you have a running car," she told him with a smile. "That will last and actually *do* something."

Nolan sipped the iced tea that was sweetened perfectly. "So it's not an attention-span thing."

She shook her head. "If I love something, I can do it for hours."

The temperature in the room spiked a few degrees. At least for Nolan. He had several ideas about how to keep her occupied for hours. The way she'd paused with a forkful of potatoes halfway to her mouth and cleared her throat before taking the bite made him wonder if she'd had a similar thought.

"You're a good cook, even if you don't really like to do it," he commented after they'd both swallowed.

"Thanks. I got better at it, but I still don't like to spend a lot of time on it. And there have been multiple times I've put something in the oven and gone out to the garage and two hours later come back to a smoke-filled kitchen and a ruined casserole."

Nolan smiled. "You love being in the garage."

She nodded, but her eyes were on her plate. "I get caught up. I'd much rather have dirt under my fingernails than bread dough."

"Why do you love the motors and stuff so much?" he asked. "Did your dad teach you?"

She looked up and Nolan wondered if she was embarrassed by how much she loved the garage and working on cars.

"My dad was always tinkering with stuff and he taught me a few things in the beginning, but I learned a lot of it by hanging out down at Bad Brakes when I was younger. Luke's dad was such a great guy. I got to know him when he fixed our family car one time. I guess he reminded me of my dad and since mine wasn't around a lot, I'd go down there after school and take cookies in, and Dan and his other mechanics thought it was cute and funny, so they'd teach me about the parts of the cars and how they all worked together. Then, when I got older, I'd hang out with the high school guys I knew that worked on cars."

Randi had always had a reputation for liking the older guys at school. Like the juniors and seniors when she was still only in junior high.

She took another bite, watching Nolan, and he wondered if she was waiting for him to ask about those rumors.

"Did you take those guys cookies too?" he asked, unable to help himself.

She'd dated Austin, a guy four years older than her, for almost a year.

She shook her head. "Those guys taught me about cars in exchange for other things."

Nolan chewed casually. Even as anger and jealousy began to simmer. What the hell had those guys been doing messing around with a girl so much younger? Hell, for some of them, it would have been a crime.

"Beer and cigarettes."

Nolan swallowed and looked over at her, aware that he was gripping his fork as if it was a weapon rather than an eating utensil. "What?"

"My parents weren't around much and with Dad out on the road, he never remembered how many beers he had left in the fridge or cartons of cigarettes he had in the cabinet. So I was easily able to take the boys stuff in exchange for them letting me help rebuild cars."

Nolan wiped his mouth and turned to drape his arm over the back of the chair. "That's all Austin wanted?" he asked pointedly.

"Oh, Austin." She nodded. "No, I gave Austin more than that. But not in exchange for working on cars."

"In exchange for what then?"

"You mean what did I get in exchange for letting him round the bases with me?" she asked.

There was a glint of mischief in her eyes that made Nolan certain she didn't feel like a victim in any way. "Yeah, what did you get?"

"I learned all about French kissing and how great having a guy's hands on me felt and how to put a condom on the right way and that sex could be really fun and great."

Nolan sat blinking at her.

Randi smiled. "I know now that I'm really lucky. Austin actually loved me, and he was really gentle and sweet and...good at it. All of my sexual firsts were with him, and they were great. I know now that's unusual and not all girls can say that." She took a long drink of her tea, watching Nolan over the edge of the glass. "By the way, I've since thanked Austin for that."

Austin still lived in Bad. He was married to a girl who graduated in the class above Randi and Nolan and they had four kids.

Nolan felt a strange emotion go through him, thinking about Austin and Randi.

Gratitude.

Not jealousy, not judgement, not indignation. Gratitude that it had been Austin to be Randi's first everything. Which was crazy, of course. He was *grateful* that Austin had treated Randi right all those years ago? Long before she was *his*...what? Randi wasn't his anything—then or now.

Still, it was definitely gratitude. He couldn't have handled the idea that Randi would have been used or manipulated by an older guy.

If she had, he would have had to confront Austin. And that may not have ended well. For one, Austin was well liked in Bad. Starting something with him wouldn't have endeared Nolan, now the outsider, to anyone. For another, Austin did heating and airconditioning work. He worked hard. Nolan sat at a desk behind a computer. He would have been hurting the next day, for sure.

"So it was good?" he finally asked when he found his voice.

She nodded. "I was young. He was more experienced. That maybe wasn't a great setup. My dad would have come unglued if he'd known. But..." She shrugged. "It was good. Austin treated me well, I liked him, and I was able to tell my friends all about sex, and I got all the awkward first-time stuff out of the way."

Don't ask. Do not ask that question. "Awkward first-time stuff like what?"

She shrugged. "Figuring out what to do with the condom after? What do you *say* after? Is it okay to tell him that you want him to do more of something? Is it okay to tell him you want him to do less of something else? Can I touch him there? How does it feel if he touches me there? Am I doing the blowjob right? What if I do swallow?" She sipped her tea again. "All of that usual stuff."

Nolan stared at her. Those were all excellent questions. The insight that women thought all those things was fascinating. But hearing Randi talk so casually about sex, so...confidently...was a major turn-on. Because she was definitely confident about it. And matter-of-fact. And it struck him that that was new.

Randi didn't talk to him confidently. Until today when they'd been talking about football. And now, about sex.

Why wasn't she always confident talking to him?

But that was it. He knew it. Now that it had occurred to him, he realized that all of those times over the years when their conversations went wacky and she seemed fidgety around him, it was because she was feeling uncomfortable.

He hated that.

And he was kind of amazed by it. Why was Randi Doyle uncomfortable around *him*?

Nolan took a deep breath and set his fork down. "So you figured everything out with Austin?"

She nodded. "Pretty much. I figured out what I like, what I don't, how to do certain things, how to not do other things."

Damn, he wanted to know every single thing she'd figured out.

"I like to think that I helped him get better too," she added. "He had a lot of experience when I met him, but practice makes perfect, you know." She sipped again.

Nolan shook his head. She was…surprising. In so many ways. He thought he'd known her, or at least all about her. He'd known her his whole life. He'd been fascinated by her for years. But he realized that he knew very little, actually. He knew what was on the surface—she was a beautiful, sweet girl with a wild streak who knew cars and football, had a reputation for liking bad boys, and who hadn't taken school very seriously. Which hadn't mattered. She co-owned a business now and drew customers from a huge radius because there didn't exist a machine with a motor she couldn't fix.

But there was more underneath, stories that he'd never heard, facts he'd never guessed. And he wanted them all.

"So cookies and blow jobs," he said casually. "Those are your specialties."

She wasn't offended. She didn't even look surprised. She grinned. "And transmissions."

Of course.

Randi was…a new story, a lead he had to follow, an in-depth investigation he had to conduct.

"But you're best at transmissions?" he asked, leaning back in his chair, settling in for a long period of discovery. He loved this part of a new story—the interview, the wide open questions, the possibility of uncovering something that neither of them was expecting.

She gave him a look. "I didn't say that."

"You're widely known as the best mechanic in five parishes."

She nodded. "Because I don't advertise the cookies and blow jobs. Or get paid for them."

"Right. So those are more like a hobby."

She laughed. "Something like that."

Nolan again appreciated how comfortable she seemed. He decided to test a theory. "I was thinking when we go to New York that maybe you'd be interested in Broadway. I could get us tickets for any show."

Something in her eyes changed immediately. "I don't know much about Broadway."

"Or we could go to a few of the museums."

She shrugged. "I can't take too many days off. Maybe we should just go for the party."

"And the shopping," he said, catching on immediately to what was going on.

"I can get something before we go," she said. "Just give me an idea of what I might need."

"Somewhere around here sells cocktail dresses?" Nolan asked, knowing that was not the case. She'd probably have to go to New Orleans at least.

"I can probably get something online." Randi pulled her foot up onto her seat and wrapped her arms around her leg. "Will we be walking a lot that night? I'd love to do heels but not if there's miles to go on foot."

He wanted her to wear heels. High, sexy, strappy heels. And a short dress that would show off her legs. And he wanted her hair up so that after the party, back at the hotel room, he could slowly take it down and run his fingers through it.

And he knew all of that sounded domineering and like he knew far too much about heels and dresses. But he'd been to enough of these parties now to know what he liked, and he wanted to make Randi feel like a princess. Deep down, all women loved to be pampered, didn't they? Even the ones who actually knew the difference between a lug nut and…other kinds of nuts.

"We'll have a car that will drop us off right in front," he told her. Even if he didn't want her in heels—which he really did—it was cold in New York. He couldn't make his Louisiana girl walk in Manhattan in February.

"A taxi?" she asked, almost looking excited.

"A limo." He was going to do this right.

"Oh." She seemed disappointed.

"You want to ride in a cab?"

"Well, it's one of the things that you think of when you think of New York," she said. "And I've never been in a cab."

"Okay, then we'll take a cab when we go shopping," he said.

"And can we have a street hot dog?"

"Um, sure." Cabs and hot dogs? She certainly wasn't demanding.

"The Rangers are in town while we're there," she said.

The Rangers. That meant nothing to Nolan. "Football?"

"Hockey."

Hockey. Something he knew even less about than football. But Randi loved her sports, and if he was going to get her dressed up and eating crab puffs, then he could watch guys skate around for a couple of hours he supposed. "I'll see what I can do."

She gave him a bright smile, and Nolan realized that there was very little Randi couldn't get from him with that look on her face.

"Do you know anything about hockey?" she asked.

"Is that the one with the black and white ball?" he asked, teasing.

She laughed. "Okay, so we'll each need a tutorial before the trip. You need to know about hockey and I need to know what to expect at a party like this."

"Guess we'll have to see each other again before that."

"Well, I hope so."

They sat smiling at each other for a long moment.

Finally, Randi said, "You want to have dessert on the couch?"

He most definitely wanted to have dessert on the couch. Her. She was all the sweetness he needed. And he wanted to have her on the couch. Then on the floor. Then maybe against the wall.

Something must have shown in his face because she said softly, "I have brownies."

"I love—"

"Or tequila."

So he wasn't the only one thinking about an alternate dessert.

Nolan stopped and pulled a breath in through his nose. He'd known that Randi had dated a lot of guys. Rumor had it that she'd been—as much as he hated the term—easy. Now, he realized that she'd simply owned her sexuality early. She clearly liked sex and was confident about it. Again, he was stupidly grateful to Austin for making it a positive thing for her. Nolan knew, somehow, that every physical encounter for Randi had been consensual. Hell, he wouldn't be surprised if she'd seduced at least half the guys she'd been with.

But he didn't want her to think that this was all there was. A book, a party and sex. He wanted more than that from her.

"I love brownies," he told her.

She studied his eyes. Then nodded. "Okay."

Nolan helped clear the table before they headed into the living room with brownies and coffee.

She set her cup on the coffee table and tucked herself into the corner of the couch facing him, her legs drawn up underneath her. She looked gorgeous. Her long dark hair was loose, her tanned legs below the hem of her skirt made his palms itch to touch, and her long slender fingers, adorned with a variety of silver rings, made him itched to *be* touched.

But it was her eyes that he kept studying. They were a whiskey brown and framed with long lashes, and they showed every single thing she was feeling. She was attracted to him. He now had no doubt, and he knew he could spend the night in her bed if he wanted to. But there was something that held him back.

New York. What it represented.

He wanted to make love to her in a thousand-dollar-a-night hotel suite overlooking Times Square with champagne in a bucket beside the bed and room service whenever they finally exhausted themselves and needed nourishment. He wanted to keep her naked except for the plush bathrobes in the room and an outrageously priced cocktail dress that would make her feel as beautiful and special as she was.

He wanted to be different. He didn't want to be another

Bad guy she made brownies for and took upstairs to the bed with the quilt her grandmother had made for her. He didn't want to be another guy who danced with her at Bad Brews and licked salt off her neck before sucking tequila out of her belly button.

Except, he wanted to be that guy too.

He was different from the other guys she'd dated and gotten close to. And he relished that. His whole life, his mother had impressed upon him that being different was a good thing and that he should aspire to more than Bad. But the truth was...he *was* different. Not because his mom told him so or pushed him to be, but because he was. He was wired differently. Now though, he knew it meant he could give Randi things the other guys never could. Because she deserved something different, something more, something special.

She'd dated Bad boys, a few from other nearby towns. Small-town Louisiana boys who knew ranching and manual labor and other blue collar work. Their social lives consisted of Bad Brews —and a hundred other hole-in-the-wall bars across the parish. The closest they came to Broadway was the high school production of *Oklahoma!* and the closest they got to the literary classics was being forced to read *Great Expectations* in English class in high school. Something most of them got through with the help of the internet and guys like Nolan.

They were good guys. Loyal to family and friends, and hardworking contributors to their communities. They made honest livings and had found their place in the world in the midst of the hills and plains, and along the bayous of Louisiana. There was nothing wrong with any of that.

But Nolan had had options that a lot of them hadn't, and he'd taken advantage of them. Now he wanted to give Randi options.

Randi was stuck here. She'd followed her interests into the mechanic shop and now co-owned the business. She didn't seem unhappy or restless, but she also didn't really know what else was out there. She hadn't been given a lot of chances to see or know or want more.

He wanted to give those to her.

And he wanted to suck tequila out of her belly button.

She lifted her cup to her lips—another body part he'd been thinking about all night—and sipped. "How did the chapter go today?" she asked.

He leaned into the cushion behind him. "Good. I have the rough draft done."

"Can I see it?" she asked eagerly.

Nolan grinned. He liked that she was excited about it. He reached for the bag he'd set by the sofa when he'd first come in. He pulled out the pages and handed them over.

She grinned at him and settled even farther into her corner, drawing her knees up so she could rest the papers on them, and started reading.

Nolan watched her. People read his work all the time. In fact, the more that read, the better for his job security. But this struck him as intimate in a way. They were words she'd helped him construct and it was about something that meant a lot to her. He wanted to do it justice and he wanted her to see herself in it.

It took her a while to read the entire chapter, and Nolan found himself perfectly content to watch her the whole time. He loved the way she nibbled on her bottom lip, the tiny wrinkle between her eyebrows that appeared and disappeared as she read, even the way she flipped the pages.

Finally she looked up. And just stared at him.

Nolan waited. After a few seconds, he shifted on the cushion. Then he frowned. "What?"

His editor at the paper barely edited him anymore. His book editor had certainly given some important input, but even then he hadn't had to rework much. Nolan was very confident in his writing and ability to tell a story. But Miranda Doyle was making him sweat.

She didn't say anything, but she stacked the papers together and leaned to put them on the coffee table next to her now-cold coffee.

Then she took a deep breath and crawled over the cushions to Nolan. She climbed into his lap, straddling him, took his face in her hands and kissed him.

She tasted like coffee and chocolate, which was right up there with tequila, and Nolan didn't hesitate for a second before opening his mouth and stroking her tongue with his, wanting every bit of her flavor. His hands cupped her hips, his fingers spreading over the perfect curves of her ass.

They kissed for several long, delicious minutes before Randi pulled back.

Nolan blinked up at her, almost forgetting what had prompted the sensual assault. "What was that?"

"That chapter isn't about the game," she said.

"It is. I recounted it quarter by quarter."

She shook her head. "But it's not about the game. It's about the people. You captured...everything about it. The buzz, the elation, the worry, the way we felt tied together, the hope and the...everything," she finished. "Is that what the whole book is like?"

It was. It was a tribute to a man who had coached in Bad for over thirty years. Who had taught hundreds of boys to play football. But it was about how much more Davis Karr was than that. It was about how, through football, he'd taught those boys to be men. And it had extended off the field and into the whole town. He'd taught parents to try harder, inspired teachers to challenge their students and themselves, the rest of the student body how to be part of something bigger than they were and how to stay true even when things weren't going as expected.

"It's about Coach," Nolan told her. "You know he's more than the game."

Her eyes got a little watery at that. She nodded. "He is. But wow, Nolan, that's—beautiful." She gave him a soft smile and stroked her hand along his jaw. "No one else could have written that and done it justice."

"It's just one chapter," he said, suddenly feeling a little choked up himself. Randi appreciated it. His words had touched her. That was almost as good as physically touching her. Almost. He ran his palms over the curves under his hands.

"Yeah, one chapter that you said you needed football help on," she said, her tone growing accusatory. "You didn't need help with any of that."

"I did," he told her honestly. "Didn't you read the part about the head cheerleader's heart pounding and her fingers tingling during the drive halfway through the fourth quarter?"

She nodded. "Yeah. That was—it's like you were in my head."

"You let me in there today."

"We talked football. And about the game, but I don't know how you knew how to describe exactly what it *felt* like."

"It was in the way you talked about it. The words you used. The look on your face. And you told me your fingers were tingling."

"You're amazing at this," she said. "Are your newspaper articles like that too?"

"Like what?"

"You interview people and tell their stories?"

He nodded. "That's always what I've wanted to do. It's one thing to report on the things happening, the events, the facts, but it brings people into the story to get the human perspective. If you can make them feel something, you can make them *do* something."

"Do what?"

"Get involved. Make a difference. Stand up for something. Speak up for something or speak out against something. Help someone." He could go on and on. Nolan reeled it in. It was hard to explain, but making people feel something, enough to want to do something with those feelings, was his calling. He knew it. And he was proud of it.

"What are your articles about?"

"People," he said simply.

"Like who?"

"Single moms trying to make it, people who are working four jobs and still not making it, military vets returning home, people rescuing animals, people starting programs, people fighting for what's right."

Randi was looking at him like she'd never met him. But she seemed very comfortable straddling his lap with his erection pressing against her inner thigh and his hands possessively splayed on her butt.

"Why do you do those stories?" she asked.

"Because we all need to know those stories. Because if we're living the same story, we need to know we're not alone. If we're not living that story, we need to know someone is."

Randi didn't say anything for a long moment. Then she licked her lips and said, "I'd really like for you to suck tequila out of my belly button."

CHAPTER
FOUR

SHE WAS horny because of a book. That was a new one.

And it wasn't even a whole book. It was one chapter. But she had never wanted to take her clothes off for a guy more than she wanted to for Nolan Winters after reading his rough draft chapter of his new book.

She didn't really read newspapers. She skimmed *The Bad News*, but it only came out once a week, and she usually knew all the news in it days before it went to print. The shop subscribed to the *San Antonio Express-News* but she tended to flip straight to the sports section and was always called away before she got through it all, and she never thought to go back for other sections.

Maybe all newspaper articles were like what Nolan had just described. And if so, she'd been missing out on sleeping with journalists all this time. It was a huge turn-on. She didn't know if it was the words, or the emotion in his tone as he told her about his stories, or what, but there was something about Nolan being able to make her feel things just with his written words that pushed buttons she hadn't even known she had.

She was a physical person. She liked to touch things, get dirty, make things happen with her hands. She'd always been that way during sex too. She responded to some dirty talk, but it was always about touch, really.

Until now. She had a definite desire to have Nolan tell her what he wanted to do to and with her in words. Written down on paper. So she could read them over and over again.

But they'd have to get up to get a keyboard or a pen and paper. They didn't need to get up for the tequila.

She reached for the lower shelf on her side table and grabbed the half bottle of Patron, the salt shaker and the plastic container of lime slices she'd stashed earlier. It was out of sight so as not to seem too overeager, but easily reached if needed.

"Prepared?" Nolan asked, sounding impressed and amused.

"Optimistic," she told him with a grin.

She felt his fingers tighten on her hips and she definitely felt the evidence that he was turned on.

She set the shaker and limes on the cushion next to them and propped the bottle in the corner of the couch next to Nolan's hip. She stripped her shirt off, leaving her in only a lacy crimson bra.

Nolan gave a low, very male groan. He lifted a hand and traced a finger over the top edge of the bra. Her breath caught at that simple first touch.

"This is so girly," he said, watching his finger as it ran over the lace. It was clear that he meant that as high praise.

"I love girly stuff when I'm not at the shop," she said.

"I've noticed." He lifted his gaze to hers. "The dresses, your hair curled, the shoes."

"You've noticed my shoes?" she asked.

"And your boots. You're a gorgeous woman who makes me hard just breathing the same air you breathe. I find everything you wear hot. But yeah, I notice the heels and boots."

"A shoe fetish?" she teased, trying not to let on that his words had wrapped around her heart and squeezed. His words got to her.

"A Miranda fetish," he said, with all seriousness.

He got to her.

Male attention wasn't new. She liked it. She loved sex, and she knew that the guys who asked her out knew that. Bad was a tiny town and the surrounding area was made up of similarly tiny towns, and word got around. But the guys also knew that she wouldn't hesitate to use her impressive right hook and that she could load and shoot a gun—and knew lots of places to hide a body and had plenty of friends who would give her an alibi. If she slept with someone, it was because she wanted to, and she didn't do it all that much anymore.

It hit her right then, looking at Nolan and acknowledging that his *words* had been part of her getting hot, that she hadn't been really turned on by a guy beyond his arms and ass in a long time. And arms and asses—her favorite parts, beyond the obvious—didn't keep her attention beyond a few dates.

It was kind of sad how many dinners she'd rushed through to get to the bedroom because that was the only place the guys really did anything for her. But Nolan...she wanted to rush to get to the bedroom, but she also hoped he'd stay for breakfast and *talk* to her.

And to think that she wanted to talk to Nolan without worrying about making a fool of herself was a damned miracle.

She reached for the bottom of his shirt and slid the cotton up to expose hard abs and a chest that made her mouth water. She loved arms and shoulders and chests. She supposed it was the football linebacker thing that had always wound her up, but Nolan was making her heart pound just as much as any of the players ever had.

Nolan seemed reluctant to let go of her, but he stretched his arms overhead and let her strip his shirt off. She let it drop on top of hers next to the couch and he immediately brought his hands back to her hips.

He was solid. Not huge, but hard and toned, and Randi took her time smoothing her hands over his pecs and shoulders, down his sides and across his abs. The muscles bunched under her touch, and she lifted her gaze to see him watching her with a hot gaze, his jaw tight.

Not taking her eyes from his, she reached for a lime and lifted it to his lips. "Open up," she said softly.

He did, and she put the lime between his teeth. He bit down gently, holding it in place.

Randi leaned in and put her nose and lips against his throat. She inhaled deeply of the scent of his soap and hot, turned-on man. Then she licked, drawing a wet path over his skin. A groan rumbled underneath her tongue, and she smiled as she sat back and shook salt over the area. Then she unscrewed the top of the tequila.

Nolan just watched, but she felt his reaction in his grip on her hips, in the hard cock under her, and the rapid rise and fall of his chest.

She tipped the bottle, letting a thin line of liquor dribble onto his collarbone and run down over his left pec. She watched the liquid as it wound its way over the bumps of his abs to the waistband of his jeans.

He was in jeans tonight. Hallelujah.

She bent her head and licked the salt from his neck, again relishing his low groan, then scooted back on his lap, going to her knees between his legs. Her hands rested on his thighs and she felt them bunch in reaction—or anticipation—as well.

The first touch of her tongue to his lower abs and his hand went to her head, his fingers bunching in her hair. She loved when guys did that.

Randi ran her tongue along the top of his waistband, loving how his fingers tightened. Then she traced the line of tequila back up his torso, slowly and thoroughly removing the tequila. She licked up the side of his neck, along the underside of his jaw, and then came to meet his mouth and the lime.

She bit into it, sucking the juice out.

Nolan released the wedge, and the next moment, Randi found herself flipped onto her back.

"My turn."

He kissed her deeply, then pulled back to replace his lips with a lime. Randi held it between her teeth, her whole body hot, need coiling deep. But Nolan decided to improvise and he reached under her to unhook her bra. The deep red lace was quickly whisked away, leaving her bare from the waist up. Nolan seemed to drink in the sight of her, then he leaned in and licked her right nipple.

Randi gasped, but as quickly as the touch had been there, it was gone, and he was shaking salt over her hardened tip. Then he slid down her body. Her skirt was bunched around her waist, her matching red panties showing, but Nolan stopped at her belly button, tipping the bottle over her stomach. The clear liquid spilled over, sliding down her side to the cushion below. Her oversensitive skin felt every millimeter the tequila touched.

Nolan gave her a wicked smile. "Now what order is it again?" His eyes fastened on her nipple. "Oh, yeah." He bent his head and licked the salt from the hard tip, but then he sucked gently, then harder as she cried out.

She arched closer, panting, her legs spread with his hard body between them. He slid down again and put his mouth against her stomach, sucking the tequila up and then following the trail where it had spilled down the side with his tongue. He licked his way back up, clearly not caring there was no tequila on the skin over her ribs or between her breasts, or on her left nipple.

By the time he slid up and took the lime from her teeth, Randi was on fire.

Nolan sucked the lime wedge, then tossed it over his shoulder, leaning in to take her mouth in a margarita-flavored kiss that definitely went straight to her head.

His hand cupped her breast, playing with the tip, rolling and tugging while she grew wetter and needier.

"Nolan," she moaned, when he moved his mouth from hers to her nipple again. "Please."

"Okay," he told her agreeably. Before sliding his hands under her skirt and stripping her panties off of her.

She still had her shoes on—red heels that happened to match her underwear, which did, incidentally, match the tiny red flowers on her skirt. She started to try to pry the back strap down her heel with the toe of her other foot, but Nolan's big hand stopped her.

"Leave them on."

Right, he liked her in heels.

"Skirt?" she asked, lifting her hips so he could pull it down too.

His eyes weren't exactly focused on her skirt, but they were paying attention to the general vicinity. "It stays too."

The pretty floral skirt was a perfect example of the feminine way she liked to dress when she wasn't at the shop. She always got a kick out of the guys who would treat her like a buddy at the shop, including swearing and talking about their latest lay, but then held doors and watched their mouths around her when she was in a dress.

Now that pretty skirt was bunched around her waist and everything below that was completely exposed to Nolan. Keeping her skirt and shoes on felt strangely naughty, and she wiggled against the cushion. "Nolan."

"I know, Ladybug."

Ladybug. Such a crazy nickname, but it made her grow even wetter. Or maybe it was the rough but affectionate tone in his voice when he said it. Either way, she was inching ever closer to an orgasm and he hadn't even touched her pussy yet.

That didn't last much longer.

"Hold this," he told her, handing her another lime wedge.

She started to lift it to her mouth but he stopped her.

"Right there." He moved her hand to rest on her left hipbone.

"What—"

She gasped as he licked a path along her inner thigh and shook salt over it. Then he tipped the tequila bottle over her mound. She felt the cool liquor trickle over her clit, adding to the wetness.

He lowered his head, licked up the salt, and then went to work getting every drop of tequila. And then some.

Randi's fingers curled into his hair and the couch cushion beside her as she held on. He ate at her, licking and sucking, drawing her clit into his mouth with perfect pressure to shoot her right to the edge. But it wasn't until he slid two fingers into her and said, "Sweetest pussy ever," that she went careening into the hardest, most satisfying orgasm of her life.

Apparently he didn't have to always *write* the words to get a reaction.

She drifted back to earth to find him grinning smugly as he plucked the lime wedge from her fingers and sucked on it.

The sucking caused the ripples of her orgasm to keep rippling and she tried to clench her thighs. But he was in the way.

"I've never loved tequila more," he said, tossing the lime wedge back into the container.

"My favorite," she said. "Absolutely."

He kissed her again. Then pushed back. Kneeling on the cushion, he unzipped his pants before standing and shoving them and his underwear to the floor.

Randi took in the sight of Nolan's hard cock. He was long and thick and firm, and she felt the ripples start again, need building just looking at him.

He held out his hand. "Ride me."

"Yes," she said on a breath, grabbing his hand and letting him pull her up as he sank back onto the cushions.

She threw her leg over him, straddling him like before. He held up a condom that he must have pulled from his pocket.

"Prepared?" she asked.

"Optimistic." The wicked grin he gave her made her inner muscles clench.

Grinning, happier than she could remember being in a long

time, she took the foil package and sheathed him, enjoying every inch of the hot steel under her hands. Before she could say anything or even get positioned, Nolan's hands were back on her hips and he was lifting her up. A moment later he eased her down as he thrust up, filling her in one long stroke.

Randi tried to catch her breath, but her body insisted she start moving, oxygen or not. She lifted and lowered herself, feeling every single drag of her body on his.

"Fuck, Randi," he said through gritted teeth.

She braced her hands on his chest and moved again, loving how his grip tightened on her and his chest rose with the huge breath he sucked in.

"Lift your skirt," he told her.

She couldn't leverage herself against his chest then, but she did as he asked, holding her skirt up. She didn't need to worry. Nolan's big hands continued to move her as if she weighed nothing.

"Damn, that's hot," he told her gruffly. "I love seeing my cock disappearing into your tight, sweet pussy. I'll never get tired of watching that."

Randi felt her inner muscles clamp down on him. Dirty talk was fine and she'd heard all the words, but she knew it was *Nolan* saying these things that made it hot and naughty and so good. Because it was more than words. She heard the way he felt in his tone and saw it in his face. This wasn't just a fuck, or a cock-and-pussy moment. This meant something to him.

"You feel so good," she managed, though her chest and throat were tight for some reason—exertion, possibly, but more likely emotions that she didn't want to deal with right now.

"Heaven on Earth," he told her. "Your body is fucking heaven on Earth."

Dang, the guy did have a way with words.

She picked up the pace though she could have happily stayed right there forever, at that leisurely rhythm, Nolan stretching her and filling her and looking at her like she was everything he'd always wanted.

But Nolan wasn't as content with leisurely. He leaned in and wrapped his arms around her waist, hugging her tight as he surged up into her, lifting and lowering her with his thrusts. And eventually that wasn't enough either. He flipped her onto her back.

"Get that pretty skirt out of my way, Ladybug," he said huskily.

She pulled it up as he plunged into her. She cried out his name, her orgasm hovering, teasing, tempting.

Nolan braced his hands on the couch on either side of her hips, locking his elbows and watched where he moved in and out of her, clearly meaning everything he'd said about never getting tired of that.

It was partly how turned on he was, how much he clearly wanted her, how much he loved being with her like this, that twisted her tighter and tighter, until finally she came apart in a flood of pleasure and heat and emotion that made her cry out his name for the second time and clamp onto him as if she could keep it all going and going.

But that was all it took to trigger Nolan's climax. He shouted her name and she wrapped her arms and legs around him, holding on tight as he came.

Neither of them moved for a few seconds, then he dropped his forehead to her shoulder and eased himself down beside her on the cushion.

She felt like they were glued together, every inch of him touching every inch of her, and she had no desire to move.

Ever.

———

Randi slipped out of bed early the next morning. She didn't want to leave. Nolan was taking up more than his share of her bed and she loved it. He was still snoring softly at five a.m. when she pulled on her jeans, T-shirt and work boots. She could have definitely used more sleep, but she had to meet her mom for their Thursday morning breakfast.

And she definitely needed coffee. Nolan had woken her two more times in the night. Once had been hard and fast and heart-pounding. Once had been slow and sweet. That was the one that had wrecked her.

That had been the one that had prompted her to wake *him* up the third time.

She wrote him a quick note and put it on her pillow, clichéd as that was, and headed to The Bad Egg. Her mom would be coming off the night shift at the hospital and just getting back to Bad. Every Thursday they met for breakfast after Katie's shift and before Randi's day started.

Randi walked into the diner and spotted her mom, already with a carafe of coffee in front of her. She slid into the booth across from Katie and immediately poured some of the brew into the cup waiting for her.

"'Morning."

"Hi, Mom." Randi gave her a grin and then drank.

"You okay?"

Randi swallowed. "Well, yeah. Why?"

"You look perky."

Randi had been getting up to open the shop at six a.m. for the past eight years. She did great work in the morning before everyone else got there. But she wasn't a morning person. Getting from horizontal to vertical was the hardest thing she did every day. And no one knew it better than the woman who'd had to haul her butt out of bed every morning for eighteen years.

"Not perky. Fine. But…normal." But she didn't feel normal. Not even a little.

She'd had sex before. She'd been with guys who'd really wanted her. But she'd never been made love to. And that was exactly what had happened with Nolan last night.

There had been sparks at Coach's party. After years of noticing each other, of dancing around any kind of relationship —physical or otherwise—of assuming they had nothing in common so they wouldn't be compatible in any way. There had been hot kissing. There had been flirting and teasing and then tequila. But she'd had no way of expecting what it would really be like with him. How amazing it would be. How…consuming.

That sounded so weird, but when he was touching her, kissing her, talking to her, moving over and in her, he was everything. There wasn't room for doubts or fears or even the ability to be surprised or amazed. He took over every thought and feeling.

And in the aftermath, *that* was pretty scary.

And surprising. And amazing.

"No, you don't look normal," Katie said. "Did something happen?"

"Something like what?" Randi asked, taking another big swallow of coffee.

"Something good, obviously," Katie said. "What is it?"

Sex with Nolan could make her perky after four hours of sleep? Huh, she might need to keep him around. She felt a smile slowly spread. She'd love to keep him around.

"There. *That*," Katie said, pointing at Randi's mouth. "What are you smiling about?"

"I'm seeing someone," she admitted.

Katie's smile was equally big. "That's wonderful. Who is it?"

Randi looked around. The diner was busy this time of day. They were a blue collar community full of people who got up with the sun. "It's brand-new. I don't really know what's going to happen. But he asked me to go to New York with him for a big party in a couple of weeks."

"Nolan Winters," Katie guessed immediately. She nodded. "I think he's had a crush on you for a while."

A few months ago, Randi would have waved that off. Or maybe she would have even agreed. But now, after Coach's party, after the last few days, after last night, she didn't like the word crush or the insinuation that it was one-sided.

"I really like him," she said. "He makes me feel…special."

Katie clearly liked that. "He should."

Yes. Randi agreed. But they all should. All the guys she'd spent time with should have looked at her like she was the best thing since someone covered a coffee bean in chocolate. They should have wanted to whisk her away to New York. They should have woken her up in the middle of the night and made love to her with their eyes locked on hers like they couldn't believe she was really there.

But none of them had. Until Nolan. And while all of that sounded a little narcissistic even in *her* head, that's not how it felt. Because she felt the same way. She'd loved not just being the object of his affection, but showing him how she felt too. The body shots, the brownies, the way she went eagerly into his arms each time he woke her—and the time that she'd awakened him —she hoped she showed him that she was just as amazed to be with him.

The waitress took their order and she and her mom chatted about her dad and how his back was feeling, if Katie should paint the kitchen yellow or white, and if Randi should wear her hair up or down for the New York party. They made their way through their eggs and waffles, discussing the touristy highlights of New York and if Randi was scared to fly. She hadn't even thought about it. She'd never flown, had never really thought she'd have a chance, so she didn't know *how* she felt about it.

"But Nolan will be with you," Katie said. "You won't be nervous if he's there."

The waitress refilled their coffees again and took their plates, and Katie excused herself to the ladies' room.

Randi sat sipping, and remembering the night before, and blushing at some of the things Nolan had gotten her to say.

Until she heard, "How long is Nolan in town?"

She straightened and glanced over her shoulder. Monica

Williams sat facing Randi's direction in the booth behind her. She couldn't see the other woman's face but she knew exactly who it was. Monica's best friend. Teresa Winters. Nolan's mother.

Randi knew Teresa, of course. She'd spent her whole life in Bad and Teresa Winters had been here, working as the receptionist at the dental office, as long as Randi could remember. She'd worked on Teresa's car a number of times as well. They got along fine. But there was something about sitting back to back with a woman whose son she'd been naked with for the better part of last night that felt funny.

"Oh, he's going back in a couple of days," Teresa said to Monica's question. "He's just here messing around in between assignments. You know he needs that downtime. He works so hard and does those in-depth stories. Every now and then he needs to blow off some steam and forget about all the demands in the city."

Randi frowned and tried *not* to lean back closer to Teresa so she didn't miss anything. Nolan was just here blowing off steam? Nolan came back every few months, and when he was in town, he made a point of seeing old friends, hanging out and catching up. And checking up on his mom. She'd been married to Nolan's dad, but he was long gone now. Nolan had been pretty young when his dad took off, by all accounts. It was long enough ago that Randi didn't remember Nolan ever having a mom and a dad at parents' day at school or in the audience for school programs and such.

Did he come home to blow off steam and escape from the job pressures? She supposed that made sense.

"I heard he had asked a Bad girl to go with him to New York," Monica said. "But no one knows who for sure."

"Oh, just for a party," Teresa said dismissively. "He's just trying to give an old friend a thrill."

Randi felt her chest tighten. Did Teresa know it was her? Did it matter? Was she right?

"I'm sure there are a million women in San Antonio and New York that would be happy to be on his arm for this big posh party," Monica said to Teresa.

"Of course," Teresa said, as if it were obvious. "But think of how fun it would be for Nolan to get to show off his new lifestyle to someone who knew him from high school. Maybe someone that didn't give him the time of day back then," Teresa said. "This is his chance to show someone from here what he's made of himself, up close and personal. I don't blame him."

"Nor do I," Monica said. "He deserves the kudos. The girl will be completely swept off her feet and her head will be spinning."

"Exactly," Teresa said. "Though how any of the girls who've spent their lives here think they can compete with New York City and San Antonio is laughable."

"It really is," Monica agreed.

"You ready to go?"

Randi watched numbly as her mother slid into the booth across from her.

Did Nolan want to show off his success because she hadn't paid attention to him romantically in high school? Was that really what this was about? But it couldn't be. If they'd stuck to tequila sex and he'd hit the road, maybe. But he'd stayed. He'd made love to her. He looked at her like she really might be the answer to everything he wanted.

He couldn't be faking that, could he?

"Randi?"

She shook herself and focused on her mother. "Yeah?"

"You ready to go?" Katie repeated.

Yeah, she felt like she might throw up her breakfast already. She couldn't stomach any more of Teresa Winters' conversation.

Randi slid from the booth and took a breath. She was going to have to walk by Teresa's table to get to the door. She could only pray that Teresa didn't know she was the one going to the party with Nolan. Otherwise, this could be very awkward when Teresa realized who was sitting right behind her.

Randi turned and smiled, first at Monica, then at Teresa. "Good morning," she greeted.

"Good morning, Miranda," Monica said.

"Hello," Teresa returned.

And Randi felt her smile die. She saw it in the other woman's face. Not only did she know Nolan had invited Randi to New York—but she'd known Randi was behind her for the whole conversation.

"Come on, sweetie. I'm about to fall asleep standing here," Katie said, nudging Randi toward the door. "Hi, ladies," she greeted the women.

Monica and Teresa smiled at her as if they hadn't just stomped on Randi's heart.

In front of the diner, Katie and Randi hugged. "Talk to you soon," Katie said. "Love you."

"Love you too."

Randi headed off across the square toward the shop, her thoughts spinning. Was Teresa right? Was Nolan just wanting to show off with the New York trip?

And if so, so what? He *had* gone on and made something of himself. She was already impressed, but if he wanted to really hammer home the point, she'd take the free trip to New York and ooh and aah over the bright lights, big city and the big important author who'd brought her. What did she care if there was a sliver of revenge to the whole thing? A dash of "look what you passed up". A hint of "you should have been nicer to me in high school".

But that was what tripped her up. She'd been nice to Nolan in high school. Always. There was no bad blood between them. He'd never asked her out, she'd never turned him down, they'd never fooled around, no one's heart had been broken.

No, he wasn't taking her to New York to rub in what could have been.

But it did leave the question—why *was* he taking her to New York? If he needed a date, there had to be a dozen other women he could have asked who would have been better choices, who knew how to dress and handle themselves at a big, fancy party.

If he'd done it to get her naked, he could now save a bunch of money on that plane ticket.

CHAPTER
FIVE

SOMETHING WAS UP WITH RANDI.

Nolan watched as she rolled underneath the car she was working on until only her legs were showing.

"We were approaching halftime. We were up, but only by three, and were only to midfield on fourth down with inches to go. Coach had to make a decision. He could punt. That would have been the safe thing. We had the lead, we had the best kicker in the state and with only a minute to go, it would be hard for the Tigers to score once Jase put the ball on the opposite end of the field."

Nolan nodded. He should be taking notes, but he couldn't pull his gaze from the strip of bare skin that showed as she lifted her arms over her head and her shirt pulled up. "But he didn't punt."

"Nope. He went for it. It was a huge gamble. If we didn't make first down, it was their ball and they were on the fifty. They had the number three running back in the state and our defense was tired and beat up."

"We were up. Why'd he go for it?" Nolan asked. He'd asked Coach the same question. He'd asked players for their take as well. But he wanted to hear Randi's answer.

She rolled out from under the car. She met his eyes. "Because anyone can play it safe. Champions do it the hard way."

Nolan loved that answer. And he wondered if Randi was the type to play it safe or do it the hard way. She seemed spunky, she seemed tough, but she hadn't ever taken any chances. She was living and working in her hometown, doing something she'd been doing since she was a kid, with the same routine and same people.

He wanted her to take a chance. With him.

It wasn't a startling revelation. But where it had been a dream, a desire before, now he accepted it. He wanted to take her with him when he left Bad. He'd made love to her. He'd poured his feelings into every touch and kiss and when he'd felt it returned, when he'd felt how much she wanted and needed his love and attention and passion, he'd realized that he couldn't leave her here. He wanted to show her the world, give her every opportunity she'd never had. She could go to school. She could be whatever she wanted, could do whatever she wanted.

"Coach said that he went for it because no one writes books about guys who play it safe," Nolan told her.

Randi smiled at that. "He's right."

Nolan nodded. He agreed with the sentiment wholeheartedly. No one remembered the safe and easy times. They remembered and appreciated the times when they took a chance and came out on top.

She rolled back under the car.

In spite of her smile, something was off with Randi today. She'd smiled at him, but it hadn't quite reached her eyes. She'd talked with him, but it was like she was explaining a football game to just some guy rather than talking about her passion with the guy who'd been the object of her passion all night.

For a second, he'd wondered if she was regretting the night before. But then he realized that she was acting hurt and uncomfortable. Not like she wished the night before hadn't happened. Not embarrassed about the way she'd called out his name and begged him and told him the most intimate thoughts in her head. Not distracted, as if she couldn't look at him without thinking about his mouth between her legs or her mouth on his cock. Not overwhelmed, as if she was dealing with some major emotions of her own after last night.

No. She was acting awkward. Again. Like she had all the times she'd tried to talk to him before this trip home.

Of course he'd asked if she was okay. To which she, of course, said she was fine.

So he was giving her space. For now.

"They went for it," Nolan said. "And made it."

"Yep, first down plus ten yards. The next play, we marched right into the end zone."

"And ended up winning the game by three."

"Right. Without that touchdown, we could have lost by three."

Nolan listened to her working under the car, studying her long legs and remembering how they'd felt wrapped around his waist as he'd thrust into the hottest, tightest, sweetest body on the planet. But more, he remembered how she sounded, breathing hard in his ear, begging for more, crying out his name —*his* name—when she came.

And he remembered how it had felt to wake up with her draped around him like she was a spider monkey and he was her favorite tree.

"Let's go to the Valentine's Day thing together."

She stopped moving. Then slowly rolled out from under the car. "What?"

"The Valentine's Day Dance. At the Community Center."

"Together?" she asked.

He smiled and stood. Crossing to where she lay on the floor, he squatted down and handed her a pink envelope.

Randi reached for the rag that was perpetually tucked into her back pocket and wiped her hands. Then she took the envelope hesitantly. She opened it and proceeded to read the sappiest card he'd ever purchased in his life. And that included the Mother's Day card he'd bought for his mom when he was seven.

She seemed to be reading it three or four times, because it took her almost two full minutes to lift her gaze from the card.

"You got me a Valentine?"

He grinned at her. "Be mine."

She swallowed and looked back at the card. "I've never gotten a Valentine before. Well, not since elementary school when everyone gave them to everyone."

Nolan liked that. And he wanted to kick a bunch of sorry, stupid asses. Like all of the men in Bad. He liked being the only person to do something special for her at the same time he hated that she hadn't had anyone crazy about her. Because that was a fucking waste.

"I've worked really hard not to be dating anyone around Valentine's Day though, so that's probably part of it," she said, almost to herself.

"You've avoided having a boyfriend around Valentine's Day?" Nolan asked. "Why?"

She shrugged. "It's a complicated holiday. Lots of expectations. Just seemed better to avoid it."

"Lots of expectations." He thought about that. He supposed it could be true. "What about this year?"

She looked up from the sappy card. "Well, you went to all the trouble of getting the card."

He nodded. "It was tough," he said lightly. And suddenly he wanted to do something tough, to go above and beyond, overboard, over-the-top for her. He wanted to work hard, to show her she was worth it.

There was a niggle in the back of his mind, almost as if he was on to something with that thought. But then Randi stood, stepped close, wrapped her arms around him and hugged him.

With his arms full of hot, sweet woman, it was hard to concentrate on anything else.

He'd been in town for a week. Randi was trying to remember the last time Nolan had stuck around that long. When he'd first started the book last summer, he'd been here for a couple of weeks. But usually, he was in and out in a weekend. Four days at the most.

She hadn't realized she'd been paying that much attention.

But apparently she had, because she knew this was the second longest he'd ever stayed in Bad since graduating.

It wasn't just his mother's words at The Bad Egg the other day that had Randi thinking about it either. It had been on her mind almost constantly since he'd asked her to the Valentine's Dance. Why was he staying? He had to have most of the book done by now. She was just helping fill in football details. There was no way he actually wanted to go to the dance at the community center. She'd never been, but the fact that she'd heard zero details about it in years past, meant it wasn't noteworthy. So that couldn't be the reason Nolan was hanging around.

She did wonder what Teresa thought of Nolan sticking around though. Especially after her comment about how he was only here in between projects. He was still working on the book. That wasn't between projects. Did Teresa know that he was here because of the book and that Randi was helping him?

It wasn't a secret that Teresa Winters thought Bad was beneath her brilliant son. Frankly, she thought Bad was beneath her whole family. Except for her no-good, scumball, lying, cheating ex-husband. All terms she'd used to describe him in multiple public places over the years.

Teresa was the most critical person in town and very few people truly liked her. Especially those who had spent their lives in Bad and loved it. She was an outsider. She'd come to town a little over thirty years ago with her husband, a Bad boy who had met her when he was going to school in Dallas.

He'd, apparently, never been forgiven for getting her pregnant right away and bringing her to Bad. He'd also, apparently, not been able to take living with her for more than six years. He'd left her behind in Bad and had never looked back.

Randi felt a little sorry for Teresa, but it was hard not to grit her teeth around the woman. It seemed that nothing was ever good enough. Teresa showed up to school board meetings, city council meetings, Chamber of Commerce meetings. And she always had a complaint. There was always something that someone was doing wrong or not doing enough of or doing too much of. Randi had heard most of it second-hand through the rumor mill, from her mother, or in the shop. Randi wasn't really the school board type. But, as a business owner in Bad, she'd witnessed Teresa's negativity at more than one Chamber meeting.

It was sad, really. Teresa had some good ideas, and she wasn't wrong when she said they could implement a summer reading program or that the businesses could all pitch in and get the sidewalk on Main repaved. But it was the way she made her suggestions and the fact that it seemed Bad was perpetually not good enough that made everyone defensive and less likely to listen.

It was hard to believe Nolan was Teresa's son, actually. Nolan was a nice guy who had always seemed to love Bad. Sure, he'd left as soon as he'd had the chance. Sure, he'd moved well beyond Bad, literally and figuratively. But he'd never seemed disdainful toward his hometown. And he came back regularly.

He just never *stayed*.

"So yesterday you told me about Marv and Dan and Chuck and Tom and how they always kept their grandsons' stats and had an ongoing competition going," Nolan said, from where he was sitting on the dirty overturned bucket again.

Randi couldn't get over that. He didn't seem to care that her shop got his pants dirty every day. He kept coming back and he'd sit on the bucket beside her work area, his notebook flipped open, pen poised. He'd been taking pages of notes every day and Randi couldn't believe it when she was going on and on about the off-field stuff that went on at football games, and she'd glanced over to find him scribbling madly.

They got off on tangents every day it seemed, and she felt bad. He was at the shop for hours every day because she didn't stick to game details. Like yesterday—she'd been talking about a big first-quarter stop the Renegades made in their fifth game of the season, and she'd gone off telling Nolan about Marv Bennett and Dan Brady and Chuck Olsen and Tom Tyler, the old guys who had grandsons who had all played for the Renegades at once. The men had sat on the very top row of the bleachers with a huge cooler of root beer and sandwiches at every single home game and made bets on their grandsons' stats. Loser had to make the sandwiches for the next game.

"Yeah," Randi said, leaning on her wrench to loosen a stubborn lug nut.

"You were saying something about Chuck and Jase, and then someone came in with a hose problem."

She grinned. A hose problem. Yeah, Audrey LeMar had needed a new water hose put in. Supposedly. Once Randi got into it, the water hose had been fine. So had all her other hoses. But Audrey had gotten the intel about what Nolan was doing at the shop every day for the gossip mill.

"Chuck Olsen didn't have any grandsons so he would have been left out of the bets," Randi said. "So he kind of adopted Jase. Jase didn't have a grandpa in the stands, so Chuck's bets were all about Jase."

Nolan was busy writing. "That's kind of nice that Chuck became Jase's adopted grandpa."

"Oh, no. No, no, no," Randi said, straightening and shaking her head. "Coach found out that Chuck was betting on him, and he went over there one night and told Chuck to stay the fuck away from Jase."

Nolan's head came up quickly. "What? Really? Why?"

"Jase's real grandpa wasn't a great guy, his mom struggled,

his dad wasn't around. Chuck's a drunk. I think Coach just didn't want anyone else making things harder for Jase."

"And Chuck stayed away?"

"Oh yeah, no one messed with Coach, especially when he was protecting one of his boys."

Nolan went back to writing.

Randi rested a hip against the front of Henry's truck. "I don't think Jase even knows that, Nolan. You can't write about it."

"No, I won't use any names or anything," he said.

"What's that got to do with football anyway?" she asked. "That's not about the game."

Nolan shook his head. "No, it's not. It's even better."

"Seriously?"

"Seriously. This is about...the world around the field," Nolan said. "The fact that so much was going on...it's like there was this whole universe of stuff happening. The field was the center —the sun—but all of these worlds were turning around it."

Randi watched him struggle to put words to the situation. But she got it. And he was right. She debated for a moment over what she was tempted to say, but finally she said, "You know those paddleball games? The ones with the wooden paddle and the ball tied to it on a string? You hit the ball out and away but it always snaps back?"

Nolan nodded.

"That's what it seemed like to me. We were all these little balls, bouncing around, but tied to football. The home games snapped us all back, no matter how far out from it we got."

Nolan just watched her for a minute. Then he said, "Can I quote you?"

She laughed and ducked her head back under the hood. "Oh, sure. Quote away." It was a cheesy metaphor. She wasn't good with words, but that was how she felt.

"So, we both know it's fair to say that football tied this town together during those years," Nolan said.

"Definitely. It doesn't matter how much money you make or

where you live or where you go to church or who you voted for
—when you're in those stands, you're a Renegade. You wear
black and silver and you root for the same thing and you're...
part of something bigger."
    She needed to stop talking. She sounded like an idiot. It was
a football game. It was crazy to get so serious about a *game*.
But she did. They all did. Nolan might not get it, but
everyone else who sat in those bleachers got it and would agree
with her.
    "And even though other things were going on in the stands
and parking lot and at the concession stand, it was still all about
the game," she said. She needed to talk about other people. That
way she could talk about the fandom but it wasn't about her
directly. He could think they were collectively nuts. Because they
were. "Like the three little old ladies who make every game a
drinking game."
    Nolan laughed. "Really?"
    "Really. The youngest of them is eighty-six and they have no
relatives playing anymore, but they come to every game and
sneak their flasks in and play their game."
    "No one else knows?"
    "Oh, everyone knows. They probably wouldn't even have to
hide the flasks anymore. They don't drive—one of their daughters drops them off and picks them up—and they don't cause
any trouble, so no one tries to stop them. Plus they watch avidly.
They have new rules each game. Like one game it might have
been a drink every time Jackson got a first down or every time
Marc punted farther than forty yards or something. Then the
next game it would be new rules."
    Nolan was grinning. "How did you know?"
    Randi shrugged. "I'm not sure. They were at every game. I
think I started listening in on their conversations because they
really knew what they were talking about."
    "And you were paying attention to them instead of the
game?"

She straightened and pinned him with a don't-ever-say-that-again look. "I paid attention to every play of every game, Mr. Winters. Don't ever doubt me."

He didn't looked chagrined at all. "Sorry, Ms. Doyle. I misspoke."

"Yeah, you did." She went back to the car.

"So what else?"

"What else? Oh, you mean the game?" She'd been talking about one of the games from the boys' senior year. "That one was the one where Carter broke free for an eighty-yarder."

"No, what else in the stands?"

She looked over at him. He seemed genuinely interested in the extraneous stories. And Randi had about a million.

"Well, there was the stuff that went on behind the stands too," she said. "That was where Jason Dawes found out that Missy was pregnant."

Nolan's eyes widened. "She told him at the game?"

"He bought her a hot dog and she ran behind the bleachers and puked her guts out."

Nolan shook his head again and wrote.

"You can't put that in your book," she protested.

"I won't use their names and I can change up the details," he said. "But this is...this is football in Bad. It's not just the guys on the field. It's everyone's game."

She nodded. "You can't be the pride and joy if no one's proud or joyful."

Nolan looked up at her. "I'm quoting you on that too."

He was funny. She went back to the truck. And kept talking.

"Okay, so second half of that game was pretty boring. No one scored and we went a solid quarter without even a first down on either side."

"Tell me more people stories," he interrupted.

"Really?" she asked as she exchanged her wrench for a smaller one.

"Yeah. I mean a lot of people know the game stats. But no one else has told me any of these other stories."

That's because they were just stories. But Randi shrugged. She liked having him here with her while she worked and if he wanted to hear stories, she could tell stories.

"Okay, well, there have been at least a dozen proposals during games."

"I knew of a couple," Nolan said. "But that many?"

"Oh easily. And then Shelly Corver went into labor and delivered her baby in the press box."

The press box was a fancy name for the wooden box that sat at the top of the bleachers where the announcer sat. *The Bad News* covered the game, but Blake Thomas, the sole owner and reporter, sat in the stands with his buddies. The local radio station, WKKP, covered the games from there though, and when it got to play-off time, a couple of television station reporters would cram into the tiny box.

"No kidding," Nolan said. "I didn't know that."

"Yep. And they named him Renegade."

"Shelly Corver named her son Renegade?" Nolan repeated.

Randi nodded. "He goes by Ren."

"What else?"

He looked fascinated, which made Randi smile. "There was the time a few years ago when a bunch of girls got into a big rumble in the parking lot."

"What?"

"Yep. They were players' sisters and they got to talking tough with some of the girls from Autre. Turned into a great big cat fight."

"You're kidding."

"Nope. Carter couldn't break it up by himself so Luke and Marc jumped in to help him. Ended up with scratches and bruises all over. Carter got a bloody nose and Marc ended up with a black eye. The girls were scrappy."

"How old were these girls?"

Randi grinned. "Eighth grade."

Nolan lifted an eyebrow. "Carter, Luke, and Marc got beat up pulling a bunch of eighth-grade girls apart?"

"Yep." She paused. "You should definitely write that one down."

He agreed. "Start over. How many little girls were there?"

———

The annual Valentine's Day party was actually a dance. Held at Bad Memories and involving cookies, punch, and lots of pink and red carnations.

It was a family-friendly event and people from three to ninety-three could be found dancing among the pink and white balloons and streamers.

The real party happened afterward at Bad Brews, though. That's where the grownups went to dance a little closer and drink something other than punch.

But Randi wasn't sure she'd ever felt better than she did folded in Nolan's arms in the middle of the tile floor in the community center, with her friends all dancing with their guys around her.

This was nice. This was sweet. Pink streamers, tiny confetti hearts all over everything, Frank Sinatra coming from the speakers.

She'd never danced to Frank Sinatra in her life. She wasn't sure she'd ever touched a pink streamer. She was pretty sure she'd never eaten a sugar cookie shaped like cupid.

This was all very romantic to her. Cheesy, clichéd, sappy. And she loved it.

Nolan had given her a Valentine. She loved that too.

She'd avoided all of this because she didn't know what to do with it. Romance meant someone thought she was special. Extra special. When someone thought you were extra special, they expected you to act like it.

She'd always felt pretty…normal. Average intelligence, nice, attractive. But she wasn't brilliant, she wasn't amazingly talented in any way, she hadn't started a charity like their classmate Melanie had, she wasn't stunningly beautiful. She was fun, social, a good friend. She was a business owner. She loved her parents. All of those things made her a nice person. But they didn't really make her extraordinary.

Nolan made her feel extraordinary.

That made her nervous. She wasn't sure she could measure up to that. Especially with a guy like Nolan. His experience with intelligent, nice, and attractive all went well beyond Bad. Randi was average in *Bad*. She didn't want to know where she fell on the whole-world spectrum. But for tonight, she was being seduced by streamers and sugar cookies and she was letting herself go with it.

This wasn't hot sex, or a drinking game at the river, or dirty dancing at Bad Brews. This was sweet and romantic. This made her feel special.

Nolan ran his hand up her spine and into her hair at the back of her head. He put his mouth to her ear. "Thank you for coming with me."

"Thank you for asking," she said honestly.

They'd spent the last few days together at the shop, talking football. He showed up, with coffee, when she opened and he left at closing time. They hadn't had dinner together. They hadn't kissed. They definitely hadn't had sex again. It was like once he'd asked her to be his Valentine, things had slowed down and gotten sweeter.

But she was kind of hoping that tonight would end naked between the sheets.

"Everyone's going to Bad Brews in a little bit," Nolan said, his low voice rumbling in her ear and giving her goose bumps. "Should we join them?"

Randi kept her head on his shoulder, thinking about the question. In the past, anyone saying "want to go to Bad Brews?"

would have been a no-brainer. But she hesitated tonight. She'd had visions of strawberries and whipped cream and satin sheets going.

Of course, she didn't have satin sheets and she'd have to stop at the store for whipped cream. She sighed. Typical.

"Sure."

"Great."

He stroked his hand up and down her back and she snuggled closer. It was a holiday. She had to remember that. One day that made people do unusual things, think about romance more than they normally would, say sweeter things than they normally would. She needed to not read anything into it. She and Nolan had some chemistry and he was home gathering some information for his book, and why not throw some hot sex with a willing girl into the mix? No one would blame him. *She* wouldn't blame him.

So she might as well enjoy the holiday too. She liked Christmas, even knowing it would end. She enjoyed her birthday every year even though it was only one day. This was the same thing.

———

Nolan watched Randi belly up to the bar with her girlfriends. Again.

The after-party at Bad Brews was a stark contrast to the community center dance. Country music blared from the jukebox, bodies pressed closer, hands wandered farther and the glasses that were being tipped back were filled with a lot more than fruit punch.

Randi was on her third Cupid's Cock shot with the girls. It was something pink and he thought he'd heard her say something about "might as well have my strawberries this way", but he was staying far away from the shot. Beer was fine with him. It looked like he was going to be her designated driver anyway.

She tipped her head back, swallowed the liquor, and set the glass down with a thunk, laughing with the girls.

They hadn't even spoken since they'd gotten here. Annabelle and Regan had pulled her up to the bar the minute they'd walked in, and she'd been drinking and talking to the girls since.

The other women were all here with someone as well, and some of those guys weren't put off by the closely formed female circle. Jackson walked right up, slid his arms around Annabelle from behind and tucked her close, whispering in her ear. She'd giggled and turned her head to kiss him, but she'd stayed at the bar. And he'd stayed right behind her. Christopher was there with Regan too, leaning an elbow casually on the bar, nursing a beer and watching the women with an amused look on his face. He wasn't intervening but he wasn't getting too far away, either.

The only guys really standing back were him and the new guy, Nick. Nick was the new doctor in town and was hung up on Brooke Donovan, but Brooke wasn't here tonight. She often wasn't. Brooke had a complicated history with the town and was *very* slowly coming out of her shell. She hadn't intended to stay in Bad past her contract date, according to rumors. Nick had apparently changed her mind. But Brooke was still a homebody.

Nick didn't seem fazed by being here alone, though.

Nolan had to admit that intrigued him. Anyone who could come into Bad as an outsider and lay claim to one of the town's most controversial characters had to have some gigantic balls. And hopefully, very good intentions. Nolan had always liked Brooke and thought the town had treated her very unfairly.

But Nick was hanging back, where Nolan was, outside the circle of friends at the bar. Nolan wasn't an outsider exactly, but he wasn't sure what he was at the moment. His girl was in there, just like all of theirs, but...he hadn't staked his claim like those guys had. It was still new. He didn't want to push Randi.

And, if things worked out with them, this scene wouldn't be the regular thing that it was for the rest of them. He and Randi wouldn't be here every weekend, wouldn't be hanging out with them all the time. They'd be in San Antonio and just coming home for visits.

He didn't know what to feel about that. He loved these guys, this town, these occasions. But it was a once-in-a-while thing for him. This was Randi's world though. He wasn't quite comfortable with stepping into her normal as if he belonged yet.

Being on the fringes of the team—a friend to all the guys but not a teammate—had often felt like this. He'd never minded. In fact, he'd stayed on the edges on purpose. He'd known he was leaving. He had bigger aspirations than Bad, so he'd kept his ties loose and his relationships light.

And he'd felt enough a part of the group. He'd been a storyteller from early on, and had been satisfied following the story of the team like he did multiple seasons of a television drama. He'd watched the personal struggles, the team's trials, the one-on-one relationships and dramas, the bonds between the football brothers, Coach and his boys, even the team and the town, as a fascinated onlooker.

Graduation that year had felt a lot like the finale episode of a favorite TV show. It was over. And Nolan found himself happy with the way it had all ended, but sad that he wasn't going to get to see it anymore.

Now he was looking in on the gang again. Some of them had left and come back. Some had stayed and struggled to find what they wanted in their own backyards. New people had been added. A few regulars were gone for good. But the core was there—the friendship and love and support. Nolan was shocked by the nostalgia he felt, watching them.

Nolan realized he'd been paying attention all along. He hadn't realized how great it all was, how everything had come full circle, until he'd started the book. But the boys who had learned about life on the football field in Bad were now the men Coach Karr had seen in them from the beginning.

He almost felt like he couldn't take credit for the book. He was just telling the stories that had unfolded in front of him. But he was very happy with how it was all coming together. And now, here in Bad Brews with two beers in him and watching the group right in front of him, he could admit that he was a month past his deadline because he didn't want to finish the book. He didn't want it to end.

"So it's always like this around here?"

Jerked from his musings, Nolan looked over at Nick, then back to the gang. They were all laughing over something Jackson had said.

"Yeah, it's always like this around here."

"Hard group to get into?" Nick asked.

Nolan thought about that, then thought about the group of friends as a whole. Christopher was a new addition. So was Lacey. Annabelle had been a classmate, but she'd been a bookworm rather than a football girl. Jase had left but had come back and been accepted immediately.

But he sensed that Nick wasn't asking about newcomers being welcomed in. He was asking about Brooke. Nolan knew she would be welcomed, though. These people were some of the best humans he knew. Loving, accepting, flawed, but aware of it.

Nolan shook his head. "No, I wouldn't say that, actually."

"But you're standing back," Nick pointed out.

He *was* standing back. But it was by choice. And habit. "I'm more of an observer," he said.

"Nolan Winters, right?" Nick asked. "You're writing that book about Coach."

"Yep. And all of those yahoos." He gestured toward the group with his beer bottle.

"Yeah?"

"Can't write about Coach without writing about those guys," Nolan said. Coach had influenced a lot of kids over the years, but none as much as the guys who'd played on his championship team.

"They seem like good people."

"They are. And they know good people when they meet them."

Nick just tipped back his beer.

"You didn't ask, but for the record, they admire Brooke staying."

Nick swallowed and met Nolan's eyes. "I don't really care what they think of Brooke. I only care what Brooke thinks of Brooke."

Yeah, Nolan liked him. Nolan nodded. "But Brooke cares what they think, right?"

Nick finally nodded. "Yeah."

"So bring her down here sometime. Let them show her that they admire her. And that they're good people."

Nick shifted. "She was going to come tonight, actually. But one of the girls at Courage House needed someone to talk to."

Nolan was aware of the shelter Nick and Brooke had opened for homeless LGBTQ teens in Brooke's mother's mansion on the outskirts of town.

"Glad to hear it," Nolan said sincerely. "Not about the teen needing help. But that Brooke was going to come to Brews tonight."

Nick gave him a grin. "I get it. And me too." He looked over at the group at the bar. "So how come you're not over there with your girl?"

"My girl?" Nolan repeated casually. But his heart kicked against his ribs.

"Randi. The gorgeous brunette—the mechanic—there in the middle who's four shots in," Nick said. "She's yours, right?"

Nolan felt the *hell yeah* rock through him. Randi was his. Absolutely. And ever since he'd given her the Valentine and seen the look on her face—how much a stupid two-dollar card had meant to her—he'd been determined to be *hers*. Not just the guy who had a crush on her, not just the guy fucking her, but the guy who took care of her and made her feel as special as she was. The guy who wanted to make her look the way that card had made her look, every day for the rest of his life.

Randi needed to be loved. And no one could do that better than him.

"Yeah, that's her," he said. "Miranda."

"So how come you're not over there with them?"

"Well, because I've been fighting being over there with them for a long time," Nolan said. "It's safer over here."

He already felt the pull—the temptation to claim a stool at the bar as his forever, to start reminiscing about old times, the urge to make a bunch of new memories to reminisce over in the years to come. It was strong here—the lure to stay, to settle down, to make a home.

"And it's just my luck that when I finally fall for a woman, it's the one in the midst, literally, of that group," he added.

Nick took a long draw of beer, watching the group, seeming to consider what Nolan had said. Then he nodded. "I've noticed that falling for a Bad girl has a way of fucking up a lot of plans."

"Your plans get fucked up?" Nolan asked.

Nick didn't even hesitate. He grinned. "Big time." He definitely didn't look disappointed or apologetic.

Nolan couldn't help but chuckle at that. "I've been trying to get Bad out of my system for ten years. I can tell you, it ain't easy. Add in a girl you're crazy about and yeah…good luck."

He paused in lifting his beer to his mouth. *Dammit.* He should listen to himself. Bad still meant something to him, even after all the years of being away, and avoiding the ties. Now Randi was making it mean even more. Seeing Randi with her friends made him happy—because *she* was happy. Taking her away from this wouldn't be easy.

"So what are you gonna do about it?" Nick asked.

There wasn't much he could do right now. He couldn't walk away from her, and that was about the only way to keep this from getting even more complicated. So he was going to cling to simple for a little longer. "I'm going to go ask my girl to dance."

Nick nodded. "Good plan."

"How about you?"

Nick set his beer bottle down and straightened. "I think I'm going to meet my girl at home."

Nolan liked that idea too. He wanted to claim Randi. He wanted everyone to know that she was his. But did he want to take her home and have her to himself? Or did he want to get right in the middle of it all right here with her for good?

Fuck. It was already complicated.

CHAPTER
SIX

"GO FOR IT," he told Nick, hoping he was able to hide his conflicting emotions.

"You too." Nick gave him a grin, clapped him on the back, then headed for the door.

Nolan took a breath and then pivoted toward the bar, but just then Randi extricated herself from the group and came for him instead.

"Let's go make out," she told him, taking his hands and starting toward the door.

He pulled her back to him, wrapping his arms around her and linking his hands at her lower back. "Hang on there, Ladybug."

He wanted to make out with her. Of course. He wasn't an idiot. Or dead. But she'd had four shots and she was in a weird mood.

She had been ever since they'd left the community center. She'd been quiet on the five-minute drive between the two places, almost seeming lost in thought, and she'd sat clear over on her side of the car. He'd been hoping she'd be plastered up against his side, frankly.

The dance had been nice. The elementary school students

helped decorate, and he'd seen the way Randi had looked at the construction paper X and O decorations on the walls and the heart shapes dangling from strings from the ceiling. She'd liked the dance. He'd liked being romantic with her. Tonight and over the last few days. It was important to him that she know this was more than sex. More than a date to the party in New York. More than football. And over the past few days, spending time together, talking and laughing at the shop, the conversation evolving from football to a multitude of other things, he'd thought she was getting that. They hadn't had sex again. He'd kept his hands to himself. He hadn't even hinted at wanting to spread her out on top of the car she was working on so he could make her scream with his tongue.

He was trying to *date* her, like a normal couple, rather than just fucking her brains out, and he'd thought she was on board with that. A girl who got stars in her eyes over a Valentine and heart-shaped sugar cookies should be on board with that.

So he wasn't sure what had happened between the door to the community center and the door to Bad Brews.

"We can make out in here," she said, pulling back and looking up at him. "Obviously." Her gaze went to the dance floor, where there was a lot more groping going on than actual dancing. "But I was kind of thinking that it would lead to a blowjob and that would probably be better out in the parking lot, if not somewhere even more private."

He couldn't *not* respond to that. Again, not an idiot or dead. But there was something in her eyes—and it wasn't whatever the liquor was that was now coursing through her bloodstream—that made him hesitate.

"Let's dance for a while," he said, turning her toward the dance floor.

"I'm done dancing. We danced at the community center," she said, resisting. "Let's go get naked."

He frowned. "Randi, you know how much I love being naked with you, but—"

"No, I don't know. I'm going to need you to prove it." She took his hand and again started toward the door.

Something about her saying she didn't know bugged him. He figured she was simply using it as an excuse to get him to leave with her, but it nagged at him.

"Randi—"

She whirled around, her eyes suddenly flashing. "I want to take you somewhere alone and let you do anything you want with me. I want to strip off my clothes and spread my legs for you. What the hell are you doing fighting me on this?"

He stared at her. With the level of the music and conversation in the place, he didn't think anyone else had heard her, but he couldn't tear his eyes away to check.

Miranda Doyle was the sexiest woman he'd ever met, and she was demanding he take her somewhere and get naked. What the hell *was* he doing?

She wet her lips. "Come on, Nolan. Let's go have some fun." She stepped closer. "At the high school newspaper office."

Damn. He'd been thinking about that since she'd first said it to him weeks ago at Coach's party. That office had been his haven. The idea of taking Randi there—and *taking* Randi there—had stirred up some major fantasies.

He'd been the paper's editor, reporter and publisher. He'd been a one-man show. Because he'd started the whole thing. There had been a school paper way back in the fifties, but it had died in the sixties when school officials shut it down when they realized that students with information were harder to control.

He'd started it back up under an administration that agreed with his assertion that students deserved to be informed about the things that affected them. But, as altruistic as that had sounded, Nolan couldn't deny the feeling of power it gave him. He had decided what got lauded and what didn't, what got attention and what didn't, what facts people had. And which ones they didn't. Sure, there was gossip. Yes, people talked. But because Nolan was a good guy, the smartest kid in school, a guy everyone liked, they trusted him and his word was final. Whatever appeared in the school newspaper was gospel.

He'd been powerful and they hadn't even realized it. He knew things—people talked to him, told him details that sometimes astounded him, shared secrets—and he chose what got into print. He'd spilled some secrets. But he'd kept even more.

He'd been the king in that office. And the idea of spreading Randi out on that old desk and making her beg and scream and come...

"Okay, let's go."

The back door to the school was, indeed, still broken. A person had to know how to get in, it didn't just swing open, but everyone knew.

He and Randi parked behind the trees about a block from the school. They ran, holding hands to the back door, and did the lift-twist-push-yank that got the thing open and slipped inside.

Nolan was nearly knocked over by the nostalgia of being in the hallways of Bad High School again. It smelled the same. It looked the same. It *felt* the same. Not caring about football had put him on the outer edge of the main group, maybe, but he'd had a lot of great times here.

They walked down the hallways, looking around, still holding hands. It was stupid, but Nolan took a second to absorb it all into his memory. He was holding hands with Miranda Doyle in the main hallway of the high school. It was a few years late, but the seventeen-year-old Nolan was pretty pumped about it.

No one was here this time of night. It wasn't like there was full-time security or even a nighttime janitor. This was Bad. So they took their time getting to the newspaper office. They stopped in front of their senior yearbook composite that hung with the others in the main hallway. Nolan instantly found Randi's photo. She'd been gorgeous back then, but as he stole a glance at her, he realized she was more beautiful now. There was a confidence and contentment about her now that drew him.

And he was proud that he'd grown into an adult who appreci-ated that stuff as much as long legs and great breasts. Because it was hard to *not* appreciate her long legs and great breasts. It was a sign he'd evolved. That was a good thing.

But he still really wanted to get her naked in the newspaper office.

"Come on," he said, tugging her down the hallway.

———

They stopped outside the guidance counselor's office. There was a tiny room, that had actually been put in as a storage closet originally, that the counselor had let Nolan convert into an office for the paper. There were no windows, not even a window in the door, and it was barely big enough for the second-hand desk they'd shoved in there. But it had worked. He'd produced three hundred copies of the paper once a week from November of his freshman year until May of his senior year.

The counselor's office was unlocked—because why wouldn't it be? They pulled the door open to the newspaper's den and Nolan reached for the light switch.

The overhead bulbs illuminated a completely new space.

The old wooden desk had been replaced with a modern style that was smaller and sleeker. The computer had been upgraded —thankfully—to a huge flat screen that left a lot more room on the desktop. There was still the typical clutter and the shelves were still there. There were even some of Nolan's old books still on those shelves. There was a huge bulletin board covering one wall that held pinned-up articles from a variety of papers. Some of the articles were his from the *San Antonio Express-News*. He was flattered. But the wall above the computer monitor was his favorite.

On the plain light tan paint were a multitude of inspirational quotes about writing, written in various handwritings with a rainbow of colored permanent marker.

Most writers regard the truth as their most valuable possession, and therefore are most economical in its use. ~ Mark Twain.

A blank piece of paper is God's way of telling us how hard it is to be God. ~ Sidney Sheldon.

It is perfectly okay to write garbage—as long as you edit brilliantly. ~ C.J. Cherryh.

I love deadlines. I like the whooshing sound they make as they fly by. ~ Douglas Adams.

And so many others. Nolan felt...something he'd never felt in this room before. As if there were people who understood him, and shared his passion.

"This is amazing," Randi said softly.

He turned to find her studying the wall of words also.

"It is," he agreed.

And it worked like a damned aphrodisiac. He would never tell her, but if Randi put on some lingerie and lay on his bed reading a book by Anna Quindlen or Anderson Cooper, he'd last about ten seconds once he took his pants off.

She moved closer to the wall and ran her fingers over the words, *Half my life is an act of revision. ~ John Irving.*

It was the hottest thing he'd ever seen. Or one of the hottest, anyway. He wanted to add something else to the list of hottest things he'd ever seen right now.

He put his hands on her hips and pulled her close, her back to his front. He rested his chin on her shoulder.

"I like football," she said, still looking at the wall.

Nolan wasn't sure why she said it, but he squeezed her hips. "I know."

"I like the game. The rules, the strategy, the whole thing. But I like football players partly because I always know what to say to them." She ran her hand over the Mark Twain quote. "He's the only one I know. I wish I knew who these other people were. I wish I could talk to people who knew who these people were."

Nolan frowned. He wasn't sure where this was going, but he sensed something strange in her tone. Almost a wistfulness.

GOT IT BAD   113

"Why don't you think you can talk to people who know those people?"

She shrugged. "I could never talk to you without stumbling all over myself. And I've known you forever. I can't imagine talking to someone I just met." She took a deep breath and turned in his arms. "I don't know if I should go to New York with you."

He shook his head immediately. "It will be great, I promise."

"Do you know why I've stuck around Bad?" she asked.

"Because you love it here."

"Because I'm comfortable here. I know everything that everyone here knows. I know more than most of them about a few things. But there isn't one conversation at Bad Brews that I can't follow."

Nolan felt his frown deepen. "You've stayed here because you're worried about not keeping up outside of Bad?"

She sighed. "I've never wanted to leave Bad," she said. "Honestly. It's not fear. It's that I like being surrounded by the same things, the same people that I've always known. I'm comfortable. I fit here."

"You can be whatever you want to be, Randi."

She shook her head, giving him a sad smile. "Come on, Nolan. That's not true. People say it and it sounds nice. But it's not true. Not everyone has the brains or the money or the opportunities to be whatever they want to be."

She was right. That was the thing. It wasn't always about desire or hard work. Sometimes it came down to dollars or having doors opened. "What did you want to be?" he asked.

She looked up into his eyes, a tiny crease between her eyebrows.

"Randi?" he asked after a few seconds.

"What I am," she finally said.

"You always wanted to be a mechanic here in Bad?"

She nodded. "Yeah. I always loved the shop. The smell of the motor oil, the conversation, the idea of taking a bunch of parts and putting them together into a big, powerful machine. The idea of being able to put my hands on something and make it work."

Nolan felt admiration expand his chest. He gave her a smile. "And that's what you do."

She nodded, but her smile fell a bit. "But that's not something I can tell people at your party. Those people make things with… words. Ideas. Imagination. Everything they do comes out of their heads."

Nolan didn't know where to start with the arguments he had for her. "That's one way to make things," he agreed. "But what you do is just as valuable. Is that what you think? That you're not good enough to spend time with them?"

She dipped her head, focusing on the middle of his chest. "I'm just not very interesting. You can exhaust my topics of conversation and knowledge in about ten minutes."

He actually laughed at that, which pulled her eyes back to his. "Seriously? We've been talking all day, every day, for the past week and we haven't exhausted your topics of conversation and knowledge."

"We're talking about football."

"You're telling me stories," he countered. "It's around the topic of football, but you haven't told me a football story in a few days."

That tiny frown was back on her face. "What? I've been talking about the championship season."

"Yes. About the people and the feelings," Nolan told her. Hell, she was practically writing his book for him. "Do you even realize that what you love most about Bad football is the people?"

She shook her head and stepped back. "What do you mean?"

"Every time you start talking about a game, you end up going to the people. You've told me about the players—what they were doing, how they looked, what they said on the side-lines. You told me about the coaches—how they made decisions, the things they said to the players to get the performance they needed. And mostly you told me about the fans—how they acted, the little dramas that went on in the stands, the emotions, the fights, the celebrations, the traditions."

Randi stared at him. "I...I'm sorry."

"What?" He gave a soft laugh. "You're a storyteller, Randi. Don't apologize. You've given me so much amazing stuff to use. This book is about more than football, and everything you've told me is about more than football. You were the perfect person to talk to. You've observed everything about football in Bad. *Everything.* Not just the plays and stats, but what it's really like to love small-town Louisiana football. You've helped me describe how a single game can be about bringing people together, about hard work and faith and friendship."

He stepped close and put a finger under her chin. "You're a storyteller. Over the past week, you've told me about when your family went camping and your memories of your grandma and how you've lived along the bayou your whole life but never driven an airboat."

She swallowed hard, looking completely stunned. "But all those people in New York aren't going to care about those stories."

"People who truly appreciate stories like them for two reasons—because they can relate to them and they make them feel bonded with someone, or because they teach them something new, gives them a new perspective, takes them somewhere they've never been. Your stories are relatable. We all have people we love the way you loved your grandma and we all have things we've never tried but that we should have. But they'll also tell them something new. Someone who's never been to a small-town football game will get caught up in your stories and feel like they're right there in the stands with you."

Her eyes widened and for the first time she looked happy. "You really think I'll be able to talk to all those people?"

"They're people." He reached for her, taking her upper arms

and pulling her close. "You love people. And you know what you do that's amazing and important and makes people love *you*? You listen. You observe. You notice the little things. If you don't feel like talking, don't talk. You'll still make them feel interesting. They'll love you."

She put her cheek against his chest and he wrapped his arms around her. He couldn't believe that Randi didn't feel confident in how interesting and amazing she was.

"But I'm not worried," he told her, running his hand up and down her back. "You've been using *words* to make me fall in love with you for the past two weeks."

She went completely still, but she didn't pull back. She didn't say anything either.

Nolan knew he was pushing. He knew it was a bad idea too. They'd known each other for a long time, but they hadn't *known* each other. He knew she was feeling the heat between them, but he didn't know what else she was feeling.

Which was interesting. He'd always prided himself on being an observer of life, insightful, astute. And more, able to tell the stories around him in a compelling way that made people want to be there. Randi had him beat in all areas.

He didn't say anything more. Just let his words hang in the air around them. Finally, seconds or minutes or weeks later, she leaned back and looked up at him.

"People have said nice things to me before, but no one has ever made me *feel* these things before," she told him.

"What things?" *You're pushing again, Winters.* But it seemed that, while he could watch the world around him and put what he saw into just the right words, when it came to Randi, he needed the words from her.

"Interesting. Appreciated. Like you don't want to be anywhere else when you're with me."

His chest tightened and his lungs protested the lack of oxygen after a few seconds. He had assumed so much with this woman. More than ever, he wanted to show her that she was amazing and that the world would think so. Not just Bad, not just him, but everyone.

"Why do you think I'm still here?" he finally asked her roughly.

"The book?" she asked.

"You." He said it firmly, looking her directly in the eye.

She wet her lips. "You came back because you're taking a breather between projects. It's just a typical visit."

He frowned slightly, but shook his head. "No. I didn't need to come back for anything but you. I wanted to come back sooner—I didn't want to leave after Coach's party, actually. And I should have my ass planted in front of my computer to finish the book that's already past due. But I'm here because I couldn't stay away any longer."

She studied his eyes, as if she was checking on how much of that he meant. Nolan knew what she'd see. It was all true. He should be locked in his office in his apartment in San Antonio right now, pushing the words out, pausing only to eat and sleep, and then only as much as was absolutely necessary. He was a month past his hard deadline and his editor was pissed. And now he was rewriting. His editor was going to come unglued when he saw that Nolan had completely reworked the five chapters the editor had already seen.

But instead of pushing the book, he was here. With Randi. Because he needed that more. He'd thought it was because he'd finally gotten a taste of her. But that was only a tiny bit of this. He'd already had her, and not only was she nowhere near out of his system, but he'd found so much more he wanted from her. And now he was revising most of what he'd already written about Coach and Bad and the Renegades. Randi was adding so much and he didn't want to get to the end. Ever.

If he could sit in her shop every single day and just watch her and talk to her for the rest of his life, he knew he'd die a happy man.

He blew out a breath. Damn. This was getting complicated.

He'd started off thinking he wanted to steal her away from Bad, sweep her off her feet, make her fall in love with the excitement of the city and take her away with him. But he'd been home this time longer than usual, and every day he was here, he added something else to the list of things he would miss when he was back in San Antonio.

Randi must have seen what she needed to in his face, because she stepped back and her fingers went to the little buttons on the front of the silky white top she wore with her dark purple skirt and combat boots. She began unbuttoning and Nolan couldn't have stopped her for anything.

He wanted Randi Doyle in this office, right now. But it wasn't about it being the high school newspaper office anymore. It wouldn't have mattered where they were. The moment had changed from a naughty fantasy to something more, and they both needed this. They needed each other.

He could feel that. She needed to be loved. By him. And that was more than he could have ever dreamed up on his own.

She slid the shirt off, letting it drop to the floor behind her. Her skirt was next. Her clothes would be covered in tiny fringes of paper and pencil-eraser shavings when she got dressed again. And that seemed very appropriate suddenly.

She stood in front of him in a silky white bra that lifted her beautiful breasts, her nipples already hard behind the cups. Her panties were also white but with dark purple flowers that matched her skirt. And she still had the boots on. So Randi. Simple white underwear with feminine flowers and lace, but skimpy enough to show off lots of smooth, tanned skin and make his mouth go dry. Pretty and sexy at the same time.

Nolan reached for her hands and lifted one to his lips.

There was another contrast represented in her hands. She wore the multitude of silver rings she always put on to go out. Very feminine rings that would be a hazard at work but that she clearly loved when she didn't have her hands in a car's guts. Her nails were freshly painted a dark purple color tonight. Nolan had noticed she always wore dark polish, and he knew it was to disguise the grease under her nails that would never completely clean up. She had some new scrapes on her hands, as well as old scars, and he kissed each one. She was a gorgeous, sweet, sexy, sassy Louisiana girl, who made everyone love her, who got her hands dirty at work and then could get good and dirty in the bedroom.

She was perfect.

After he'd kissed all of the marks on her hands, he tugged her closer and kissed his way up her arm. Goose bumps broke out on her skin and a shot of satisfaction went through him. He kissed over the top of her shoulder and to her neck. Her head fell to the side and she gave a happy sigh as his lips met the sensitive skin just below her ear. His other hand cupped her head and he kissed along her jaw to her lips. The first kiss was sweet, lips only, and he absorbed the way she seemed to melt into him with only that little bit.

Nolan pulled back and looked down at her. "I want you. Spread out on this desk, right now."

She nodded and swallowed. "Anything you want."

Something about the words made him pause. "I want what you want."

She gave him a smile that was cute and sexy as hell at the same time. "Well, this is your fantasy spot," she told him. "We can do mine another time."

Another time. He liked the sound of that. But he couldn't resist asking, "Where's your fantasy spot?"

Her smile grew. "Fifty yard line in what is now Davis Karr Field."

Of course it was. He chuckled. "Not the end zone?"

"I like the fifty better," she said.

He couldn't resist running his hand up and down her arm. "Why?"

She trembled under his touch. "Because the fifty is where anything can happen, things can go either way, and it's all about who wants it more. It's all about possibilities and desire at the fifty."

Nolan stared at her.

"What?" she asked.

"You really think you don't have a way with words and imagination?"

She blushed slightly and dipped her head.

"Oh, no." He tipped her chin up. "I *will* find a way of making that fantasy come true. I want to be a part of that."

She gave him a small smile.

God, how did this woman not know what she did to him? What she had inside of her?

She reached behind her and unhooked her bra. As it fell away and he drank in the sight of her breasts, his chest tightened. Then she hooked her thumbs in the top of her panties and pushed them to the tops of her boots.

"Boots on," he said gruffly as she started to wiggle out of one.

Her smile grew. "The city boy likes my boots?"

"Fuck yeah." He picked her up and set her on the edge of the desk and pulled her panties off over the boots. "You might have to keep them on in bed forever." He looked directly into her eyes, in spite of her being completely naked and only inches away. "And before I lick you to your first orgasm of the night, you should know that I'm in love with you."

CHAPTER
SEVEN

RANDI FELT heat and something so much more—something happier and exciting and *right*—rock through her.

Nolan had just officially said that he was in love with her.

Nolan Winters, who had a huge life in San Antonio, who had left Bad and done amazing things, who was a *New York Times* bestselling author and spent his time with people who made the news—literally—and who wrote books that taught and influenced and challenged other people, was in love with *her*.

She blew out the breath that had lodged in her chest and then stretched her legs out, wrapping them around his hips and pulling him in. She took his face in her hands and kissed him, long and deeply.

She didn't let him go for almost three full minutes. When she did, she told him honestly, "I'm in love with you too."

She hadn't realized it until he'd said it. Or maybe she hadn't let herself really think about it, because it seemed ridiculous that Nolan would feel the same way. But now, she felt it. He'd been sweet, not pushing, not trying to get her clothes off at every turn, but he'd spent time, really talking and listening. She'd never had a man's ongoing attention like that. At least not without sex involved. And sure, he needed help with his book, but they'd gone off on so many tangents, she wasn't sure she'd given him anything useful in days. But tonight he'd truly made her feel appreciated and interesting.

Nolan didn't seem to know what to say to her declaration and she smiled, thinking that the word man didn't know what to say.

So she let him talk with his body. "Love me, Nolan."

He let out a long, shaky breath, and then he kissed her.

And it was unlike any other kiss of her life. He held her head in his hands, his lips taking over every thought in her mind. The kiss was deep and hot, then sweet, then soft, then hungry. It felt like they went through every emotion in that one kiss, and Randi felt the eagerness to be close to him, to be a *part* of him, climbing with every second.

Finally, his hands went from her head to her ass and he brought her up against him. He was still dressed and she was totally naked except for her boots. The rough denim of his jeans rubbed against her clit and she whimpered as the sensations ripped through her.

He let her up for air, but dipped his knees so he could take a nipple into his mouth. He didn't ease in. He sucked hard and Randi gasped, pleasure streaking from breast to clit.

She gripped the back of his head, arching closer, and rubbing against the denim-clad length of his cock.

"Lie back," he said huskily, lifting his head.

She complied immediately. She lay back on the desk, feeling the folders and paper shifting underneath her. She really hoped the kids working in here wouldn't mind the wrinkles on Monday. Not that they would know what caused them—she giggled thinking about it.

"What?" he asked, his gaze hungrily taking in the view.

She was on her back, her legs spread on either side of his hips.

"Just hoping I'm not ruining anyone's homework."

He gave her a wicked grin. "I'll leave a note explaining what happened. No one will mind."

She laughed. "I don't think that will be necessary."

"Oh, come on. I want everyone in this town to know I nailed Randi Doyle in the newspaper office." His gaze tracked over her again and he ran a hand up and down her leg. "I want to give my fellow nerds hope."

She chuckled and shook her head. "Well, be sure to tell them not to assume things because of a cheerleading uniform or just because she doesn't like math class."

"Is that what I did?" he asked.

"Isn't it?"

He gave a nod. "Yeah, maybe."

"I can tell you, in high school, I could have used a lot of..." She trailed off when she realized how she'd been about to finish that sentence.

He squeezed her calf. "Tell me."

She knew she could say anything to him, somehow. They'd only really been getting to know each other for a few days, but it felt like so much longer. She'd told him things she'd never told anyone else, and tonight he'd convinced her that all of that had actually made him fall for her.

She took a breath and said softly, "You."

His hand stopped moving for a second. "Me?"

She nodded. "I could have used a lot of *you* in high school. The way you look at me. The way you make me feel."

His eyes darkened and he leaned in, one big hand wrapped around her calf, bracing his other hand on the desk beside her hip. "How do I look at you and make you feel?"

"Special."

Nolan didn't say anything to that for a moment. He just looked at her, heat and hunger in his gaze.

Then he dropped to his knees between her legs. The first touch of his tongue was on the ladybug tattoo on her hip that she'd shown him so long ago at the football party. The second was firm and exactly on the spot where she was aching for him. He licked over her clit and she arched her back, gasping. He didn't go easy. He licked and then sucked, sliding two fingers into her. The pressure was perfect, but it was the words that made her melt and wound her tight at the same time.

"So beautiful." "Perfect". "Everything I've ever wanted." "Worship you". And her favorite, the one that sent her flying, "Love you."

Randi was still gasping for breath when Nolan rolled her to her stomach as he stood.

The newspaper underneath her crinkled and slid with her as her feet touched the floor and her stomach and breasts pressed into the desktop.

"You have newsprint on your ass." Nolan stroked his palm over the curve of her butt that had been on top of the newspaper.

"Oh, crap." She started to get up.

"Sexiest fucking thing I've ever seen." His voice was rough.

She looked over her shoulder at him. He looked completely turned on, his eyes still on her butt. She grinned. "Next tattoo is going right there. Script font. Maybe one of the quotes from the wall."

His eyes found hers and he was completely serious when he said, "Words are powerful."

She felt her breath catch at the intense look in his eyes. She nodded.

"Sometimes you can say everything you need to say with just one of them."

She swallowed and nodded again.

"You know what I want your tattoo to say?"

She shook her head.

"Mine."

Randi felt such a wave of emotions that tears welled up. One word and he had, indeed, said so much. And made her feel so much.

She had no words of her own.

So she used what she had. She turned and reached for him, sliding his shirt up his body and over his head. She unbuttoned and unzipped his pants, freeing the steely-hard erection that was all for her.

Then it was her turn to go to her knees.

Nolan didn't try to stop her. His fingers tangled in her hair as she wrapped her fingers around his cock and stroked, then leaned in to take him into her mouth. She licked base to tip, before sucking hard. His deep, very male groan made her whole body pulse with awareness. Yeah, *mine* definitely worked for her too. She'd tattoo the word all over his body.

He let her work him for a few minutes but before she was ready, he tugged her to her feet and took her mouth with his in a hot kiss. Then he turned her and pressed her down onto the desk, her breasts against the newspaper. He moved in behind her and she heard the sounds of a condom being opened. Then his hands were on her hips again and he thrust deep with one powerful stroke.

"*Yes*, Nolan."

"Damn, you're perfect. So perfect." He moved, thrusting in and out in long, slow glides.

Randi felt electricity zapping along every nerve she possessed, her awareness condensed to this moment with this man—the feel of the desk, Nolan's hard body behind her, his fingers curling into her hips, the sound of the papers rustling and their heavy breathing, the sexy, sweet words he uttered, the hoarseness in his voice, her own gasps and moans.

He slid a hand forward to cup her breast and tug on a nipple, and she felt the ripples of pleasure deep where she clenched around him.

"Fuck yes," was his answer.

Then he slid the hand lower, stroking over her clit. She gasped and pressed back harder against him. He did it again and again, his touch winding her perfectly until he leaned in, his chest to her shoulder blades, and said gruffly, "Come for me, Ladybug."

She felt the shudder of pleasure go through her and on his next thrust, she came apart. He thrust twice more, then tensed and groaned her name as he came, buried deep.

They stood, panting together for a few minutes. Randi was pretty sure she could stay draped over that desk for the next few weeks and her legs would still feel like jelly. Eventually Nolan stood and pulled out. She turned her head, watching him deal with the condom and pull up his pants.

"I think this newspaper has become a part of me," she said.

He looked over with a grin. "Let's see." He tugged her to standing and sure enough, the newspaper came too. He peeled it off of her skin carefully. She had ink smeared on both breasts and her stomach. "I didn't even know I had fantasies about you covered in newsprint, but damn."

She laughed and nudged him back so she could reach for her clothes. "You're such a nerd."

He caught her hand against his chest and brought her in for a kiss. "Yes. The nerd who just made the head cheerleader scream in ecstasy."

Well, she couldn't argue with that.

They both dressed and Randi opened her mouth to invite him to her house for the night—when they heard voices on the other side of the door and getting louder.

Their gazes collided and Nolan lifted a finger to his lips. He reached over and shut the light off. The room plunged into total dark and Randi felt disoriented for a moment. Then she felt Nolan move in close and wrap his arms around her. She hugged him back, grateful for the anchor as they waited.

There was a quick flicker of light under the door, clearly from a flashlight, a moment before the outside office light came on.

"You didn't go out the back door though, right?"

It was Carter Shaw's voice. One of the local cops. Randi cuddled in closer to Nolan. Not because she was afraid of

Carter's badge. More because she could already see Carter's shit-eating grin if he caught them. And she knew the story would beat her to work in the morning.

One thing about being the only girl in a garage full of guys who treated her like a sister—they treated her like a sister. Teasing and all.

"Of course not. Went out the front."

And that was Jackson Brady's voice. The outer guidance counselor's office was his.

Randi dropped her forehead to Nolan's chest. Great.

Nolan chuckled softly and stroked his hand up and down her back. She loved when he did that. She felt so cared for. Nolan had a way of making her feel like she was the most precious thing in the world. She could really get used to that.

She could also really miss that when he was gone.

She tamped down that thought. Yes, he lived in San Antonio. But it wasn't France. Or Mars. And he loved her. There had to be a way to work things out. They'd get to that.

"Well, we looked all over the building. Nobody's here. Maybe the back door blew open," Carter said.

"Yep, guess so. Just thought it was worth checking out when I saw the door open." There was the sound of a chair scraping on the floor, then a creak.

Was Jackson sitting down at his desk?

"Thanks for coming right over," Jackson said. "Wanted to get some work done tonight."

"No problem," Carter said. "Slow night."

Randi heard Jackson laugh. "It's Bad. Slow night is a typical night, right?"

"You got it."

"Want some coffee?" Jackson asked.

"That'd be great."

Randi lifted her head then thumped it against Nolan's chest again. They were going to sit around and have coffee? And then

Jackson had some work to do? She and Nolan could be stuck in here all night.

She heard them moving around, water running and then coffee mugs clinking.

It was really dark in the newspaper office, which was, technically, a converted storage office. It was also hot. It was a small space in which they'd worked up some major body heat and it didn't have any ventilation except for the crack under the door. Randi stepped back from Nolan slightly, thinking that would help.

Twenty minutes later, she had her boots off, her shirt off and was sitting on the edge of the desk in her skirt and bra, fanning herself with a folder she'd found on the desk.

Nolan had stripped his shirt off too and was sitting on the floor next to the desk.

Randi would have given a kidney for a glass of water.

And Jackson and Carter continued to chit-chat and drink coffee right outside the door. Jackson was the guidance counselor, so he had a big comfy couch in his office, to make students more comfortable while they got guidance and counseling, and she imagined Carter lounging on the sofa, his feet up, drinking coffee and waiting for someone to commit a crime.

That could be a very long wait.

"So Nolan and Randi, huh?" Carter asked. "That's great."

Randi perked up and stopped fanning with the folder. She heard Nolan shift on the floor as well.

"Yep, Annabelle says Randi's crazy about him," Jackson said.

Randi frowned. She had not told Annabelle that. She hadn't told anyone that. Though she could admit that it might be obvious to her friend. Annabelle knew her well.

She jumped slightly as she felt Nolan's hand wrap around her ankle. Yeah, okay, she was crazy about him.

"No kidding? Well, that's awesome. Nolan's a great guy, Randi's a great girl. I'm happy for them," Carter said.

"Randi is great," Jackson agreed. "We went out in high school."

Randi rolled her eyes. They'd gone out for maybe two months a lifetime ago. It had been high school. It had meant nothing. She didn't want Nolan to have the wrong idea. She'd have to tell him later that it had been nothing with Jackson.

She felt his thumb rub up and down the front of her ankle and foot. She wasn't sure if he meant it to be reassuring, but it was. He didn't care that she'd gone out with Jackson a couple of time.

"I dated her too," Carter said.

Randi rolled her eyes again. Barely. She and Carter had had three dates and she wasn't sure one really counted, since all they'd done was talk about the upcoming football game against their rivals, Riverbend.

Nolan's thumb kept moving, slow and steady, and she breathed in and out. Her past boyfriends didn't matter. Jackson and Carter certainly didn't. They hadn't been boyfriends. They'd been guys she'd had a meal or two with.

"Because Coach asked her to go over the game film with you," Jackson said.

"He asked her to go over game film with a lot of people," Carter pointed out.

That was all true. When there was something Coach really wanted the guys to take note of, he often had Randi talk them through it. He said they tuned him out. Randi had since suspected that it had actually been because Coach knew how much she loved going over film and that it had made her feel important. Coach hadn't only been influential with the guys on the team. Anyone who crossed paths with him felt better about themselves, and when he noticed someone needed something, he provided it. Subtly. Often without that person even knowing it. But Randi had always suspected he had her number, and he specifically found ways of making her a part of the team as much as he could.

"She never went over film with me," Jackson said, sounding smug.

Again, Randi couldn't protest. Jackson had been a natural. He'd been a running back and his ability to read a defense was amazing. It wasn't something that could be taught. She'd loved watching him play. She knew that was why she'd said yes when he asked her out. But they'd fizzled out quickly. Probably because her main attraction to him was how he could pluck an impossible catch out of the air and take it in for six. But their two months of dating had been fun.

"Did she help you with some of your moves, though?" Carter asked.

"We talkin' football?" Jackson asked.

"Nope."

"Then yeah, a few."

Randi sighed. She could *hear* Jackson's huge grin. She also felt Nolan's hold tighten around her lower leg. She and Jackson had never slept together. But yeah, okay, they might have made out a little. Jackson was a really good-looking guy. Who played football and liked to talk to her about it. That meant he met all of her criteria—goodlooking, played football, talked football. But they'd never been serious and she was going to be sure Nolan knew that. As soon as she could speak out loud without getting arrested.

"We didn't just sit around talking football either," Carter said.

Had their voices gotten louder? Randi frowned slightly.

"Well, of course not. I mean, Randi's the best to talk game with but she's way too gorgeous to *only* talk football," Jackson said.

Yes, their voices were definitely louder. As if they'd moved closer to the door. Crap, were they coming in here?

"And any guy who wants to sit around for hours and just talk to her is crazy," Carter said.

"Well, Nolan's faking most of that," Jackson said.

Randi sat up a little straighter. Nolan's hand tightened around her ankle briefly.

"No kidding," Carter said.

If Randi didn't know better, she'd think they were standing on either side of the door, leaning against the wall as they talked. She frowned. What was going on?

"Nolan knows a lot about football," Jackson said. "I think he's faking the whole thing about needing help with the details so he can hang out with Randi."

"Makes sense," Carter said. "He's a smart guy and it's just football. It's not like he couldn't figure it out himself."

Randi frowned. It was true. With some study, almost anyone could learn the game. Especially a guy as intelligent as Nolan. But Nolan himself had said that what she'd been giving him was about more than just the technicalities of the game.

"He *is* a smart guy," Jackson agreed. "But if he's as *brilliant* as I think he is, he'll watch the tape of the game our senior year against Autre with her."

Randi grimaced. The game against Autre had been rough. Autre had come to town wanting to take the top-rated Renegades out. No matter what. And the refs had sucked. A few fans had been thrown out of the game by security. And she'd made history. It was the first time anyone could remember that the head cheerleader—or any cheerleader—was one of the people escorted out.

But the refs had *sucked*. Randi didn't regret a single thing she'd yelled at the guys in stripes. Or at the dickhead group of dads on the other side who didn't know pass interference from pancakes. She also didn't really regret that some of the junior varsity guys had needed to step between her and one of those dads who thought he'd come to their side of the field and tell the "little girl" a thing or two about football. Two of the JV players had needed to carry Randi out to the parking lot because she'd been about to go at the guy. And she knew how to throw a punch.

Their high school principal, Mr. Whitacre, had agreed with her about the refs. He'd had to give her three days of detention for unsportsmanlike conduct, per school policy, but they'd spent the time in his office rehashing the game and every screwed-up call.

"Randi's beautiful, but when she gets riled up about football, she's gorgeous," Carter agreed.

Randi felt the pleasure of the compliment go through her, right on top of the flush of uneasiness. There were some other stories they could tell. Just as she got riled up over bad officiating and bad play-calling, she could get just as worked up over brilliant plays and victories. Nothing got her blood pumping like a great Hail Mary or a trick play that worked or a well-executed onside kick. Parties after her team won were some of the most fun she ever had. She was funnier and cleverer with post-game adrenaline pumping. She was even a better dancer when her team won.

Jackson gave a small laugh. "I know it. Remember the Super Bowl party at Brews last year? She was all riled up over that call in the first half? I swear, half the guys there wanted to—"

Yep, like *that* story.

Randi was off the desk and yanking open the door before Jackson could finish his sentence.

"Okay. Enough," she interrupted. She'd been riled up about the call, all right. She'd gotten into a huge argument with Kyle Simpson about it and they'd ended up naked together later that night. Football was an aphrodisiac for her. She couldn't help it.

And she'd been right about Carter and Jackson leaning on the wall beside the door. They both straightened with big grins, not at all shocked to see her. Though they might have been slightly surprised that she was in only her bra.

She narrowed her eyes, realizing what was really going on out here. "You knew we were in there."

They both laughed. "I saw you break in," Carter said.

She felt Nolan move in behind her and then her shirt flop over her shoulder.

"Hey, guys," Nolan said easily.

"*You* knew they knew we were here the whole time?" she asked, shrugging into her shirt and buttoning it up.

"No. I figured it out when they started talking about making out with you in high school," Nolan said, drily.

"So you were out here, yakking and drinking coffee and screwing around, knowing we were in there in the dark, sweating our asses off?"

"We thought the sweating part was over," Carter said.

"Not *that* sweating part," Randi said. "It's hotter than hell in there."

"Good reason to get naked," Carter told her with a shrug.

"But you saw us break in?" Randi asked him with a frown.

"Give me some credit. I'm a good cop." He gave her a big grin.

"You mean you were waiting for your root beer float at Bad Gas," Randi said. Carter loved the root beer floats at the convenience store that happened to sit across the road from the high school.

"But I noticed and followed up," Carter said, still grinning, unaffected by her critique of his detective skills.

"And you didn't come in and stop us right away?" Randi asked him.

"Bro code," Carter said, shooting a grin at Nolan. "Had to give Winters some time."

"And he had to wait for me to get here anyway," Jackson said.

"Why did *you* need to be here?" Randi asked.

"Because I'm enjoying this immensely."

She huffed out a breath. "We almost sweated to death in there."

"Good for you," Carter said, grinning at Nolan again.

"Not because—never mind," she said. "Are you going to escort us out?"

"Nah, you can find your way," Carter said, setting his coffee cup on Jackson's desk. "Let's go, Brady."

"'K." Jackson pushed away from the wall. "Be sure you turn the lights off." He ambled toward the door.

"Really? You just came in here to give us a hard time?" Randi asked.

"Yeah," Carter said with a shrug.

"And because I now know something about you that Annabelle doesn't know," Jackson said. "I love that."

Randi sighed. She was going to get called for a girls' night soon, where Annabelle, Regan, Priscilla, and the others were going to want to know everything about her and Nolan. Not that she minded. She had listened to many of them talk about their guys and falling in love and the confusing feelings that went with it. And now she knew how hard it was to put all of it into words.

Jackson and Carter headed into the hallway outside of Jackson's office. "Oh, hey," Jackson said, turning back. "Don't leave any condoms or wrappers laying around. These are impressionable kids."

"And they'll think they're yours?" Nolan asked.

Jackson faked looking affronted. "I would never."

"You would never get caught, maybe," Nolan said.

Jackson had been a wild child, but he'd been impressively good at getting out of things.

Jackson chuckled. "I meant I would never use that tiny office. Annabelle and I need more room than that. We stick to *my* desk."

He left the office, pulling the door shut behind him.

Randi turned to look at Nolan. He was shaking his head over Jackson. She couldn't help her big grin. "I never slept with either Jackson or Carter."

Nolan nodded. "I know."

"You do?"

"Are you kidding? If you had, those guys would have been telling everyone."

Randi gave him a little frown. "What?"

"Randi, every guy in high school wanted you. Taking you out was big bragging rights. Getting you to talk about something other than football was a huge accomplishment. Getting you to stop talking at all long enough to get a kiss was big time. More than that—" He shrugged. "Everyone knew that you were special. They would have been talking."

She didn't think that was true at all. But she felt warmed by his assessment. "And no one ever made stories up?"

He shook his head with a smile. "It's Bad. Everyone knew everything. They could have tried, but your girlfriends, who knew the truth, would have kicked their asses. And then your girlfriends' boyfriends would have kicked their asses again. You have a very loyal group of friends and everyone liked you—no one wanted to make stories up. They wanted to make stuff come true." He reached out and drew her near.

And she went willingly into his arms.

"And don't think for one second that I don't realize how amazing it is that I got you to fall for me."

She tipped her head back to look up at him. "Not amazing. I might have almost failed geometry, but it turns out that I'm pretty smart about the things that really matter. And being with you really matters."

CHAPTER
EIGHT

"WHAT DO YOU THINK? This one or the blue?"

Randi stepped out of the dressing room and executed a three-sixty for Annabelle, Priscilla, and Regan.

"Oh my God." Cilla stood from her chair and came forward. "This one."

Annabelle was nodding. "Definitely this one."

"I don't know. Blue is safer," Regan said.

Randi looked over her shoulder at the mirror. The white dress hit her at mid-thigh. It crossed over one shoulder, leaving the other bare, hugged her breasts and waist and then flared at her hips. It made her tan look amazing and she loved the light, floaty material. She knew that people were sometimes surprised by how girly she could be, but just because she knew CCV valves, didn't mean she didn't also know tulle and chiffon.

"The blue is safer?" Randi asked Regan. She liked the blue dress too, but there was something about the off-the-shoulder white that she really loved.

"You won't make it out of the hotel room on time—or at all—with the white one on," Regan said with a grin.

Randi laughed. She could live with that. "Well, it's not *my* agent and editor at this party. Guess Nolan will have to risk it."

The girls had been talking about the party in New York, and Randi had been asking for opinions of some dresses she'd found online. They'd all finally agreed on one thing—she needed to order a bunch and try them all on to really make a decision. Regan and Annabelle had headed downtown and asked Corinne, who owned the shop where everyone bought their jeans and boots, if she'd be willing to order some things in. Corinne had been excited to do it and today was dress-up day.

"Okay, so all for the white?" Annabelle asked.

All the girls, including Randi, raised their hands.

"Awesome. Now shoes." Randi was equally excited about the heels Corinne had insisted on ordering as well.

The three girls headed up to the front to find Corinne, and Randi twirled in front of the mirror in the changing area. She really did love this dress and she couldn't wait for Nolan to see her in it.

She was surprised by how excited she was about the New York trip now. She'd been worried, she could admit. New York was as different from her usual life as she could possibly get. But now, with everything that had happened with Nolan, his reassurances that she would be fine in conversation with these people, but even more, how much *he* clearly loved being with her, made her feel so much more secure. It didn't matter what the editor and agent thought of her. Nolan loved her the way she was. She'd be herself and trust that they would too…or that it wouldn't matter if they didn't.

She watched the skirt float up and then settle as she stopped turning. She checked the dress out again, running her hand down the front of the bodice. But when she lifted her gaze, something caught her eye in the mirror.

No, nothing something. Someone.

Teresa Winters.

Randi took a deep breath and turned. There was something in Teresa's face that told Randi Teresa wasn't at all surprised to see her. In fact, she looked ready for a fight.

"How did you know I was here?" Randi asked.

"Beverly told Monica that she heard Corinne was ordering some dresses for a big party in New York. It didn't really take much to figure this out."

"And you asked Corinne to call you when I came in for the fitting," Randi guessed.

Teresa gave her a small, fake smile. "Don't you love small-town life?"

Randi lifted her chin. "Actually, yes, I do."

Teresa's smile disappeared. "I know."

"And that's the problem, right? I'm not good enough for Nolan. Just like Bad isn't good enough for Nolan."

"Right."

Randi blinked. Not even a bit of subtly or hesitation. Okay, so that meant she didn't have to try to be nice either. "I make your son happy, Teresa. That should matter to you."

"Nolan had a crush on you in high school. Now he's just caught up in having a chance with you."

Randi laughed at that. "Wow, you almost gave me a compliment. You better be careful."

Teresa frowned. "If you care about him, you'll end this. You know how talented he is. He deserves a chance to do everything he can with that. And you know that chance won't come in Bad."

Randi didn't reply right away. She heard what Teresa was saying. And she wasn't wrong. "Nolan is writing a book. He can do that anywhere. He can fly to New York when he needs to just like he does now."

"And what if the book doesn't do well? What if he only has two books in him?" Teresa asked. "He has to keep his job in San Antonio."

"There are stories here," Randi said. But the niggle of doubt grew with Teresa's words. It wasn't like Randi hadn't thought of all of these things. But she'd been ignoring them. Because two weeks was too short of a time for any of it to matter, for one thing. For another, she was assuming a lot in thinking that Nolan was thinking about moving back to Bad.

"And who is he going to tell the stories to?" Teresa asked.

Strangely, her voice lacked any disdain. She almost seemed sympathetic.

"Teresa—"

"Go to San Antonio with him."

Randi frowned. "We fly out of San Antonio on Saturday morning."

"I mean after. When he goes back."

Randi felt her heart rate speed up. "What?"

"I saw you together at the Valentine's dance," Teresa said, hugging her arms to her stomach. "I saw how he looked at you."

Randi wet her lips. Over Teresa's shoulder, she saw the girls coming back with shoes. Regan gave her a look that said "do I need to kick someone's ass?" Annabelle gave her a look that said "are you okay?"

She tucked her hair behind her ear and said, "How did he look at me?"

It was more for her friends than for Teresa. They got the message and moved back out of sight. But she knew they were there, listening, ready to jump in if she needed them.

"Like he never wanted to be anywhere else."

Randi's breath caught. God, she wanted that to be true. So much.

At least, she thought she did. She wanted him to be where he needed to be. Where he was happiest.

"He's in love with you," Teresa said.

Randi nodded. "Yes." No matter what else, she believed that.

"He's never been in love before. Not with a woman, anyway," Teresa told her. "He's been in love with his work for years."

Randi nodded again.

"Don't make him choose," Teresa said. "Don't make him pick between you and his work."

Randi understood what Teresa *wasn't* saying. And it warmed her, even as it made her stomach hurt. Teresa thought Nolan would choose Randi. Over his work, over his passion.

She'd never been that important to someone before. She'd never been the thing that was the biggest and best part of someone's life. But she couldn't just absorb all of that and enjoy it. Because she loved him too. And she couldn't ask him to give up what he loved.

Teresa continued when Randi didn't respond. "So just go to San Antonio with him. Let him have both."

"I..." Randi shifted her weight. "My work is here. This is my home. My family and friends are here."

That was when Teresa's eyes hardened. "You're a mechanic in a backward hick town in the middle of nowhere. This is your chance to get out and do something great too. Please tell me that my son is smart enough to fall in love with a woman who is smart enough to recognize an opportunity when she sees it."

Randi had to admit that it seemed like Teresa had a point. But Randi was in Bad because she wanted to be. The irony was that over the past two weeks, talking with Nolan and telling him the stories of Bad, had made her love her hometown all over again. And had made her sure that this was where she wanted to be. For good.

She wanted to live here. She wanted to be a part of this community. She wanted to watch the cars and trucks drive up and down Main from the window at Bad Habit and know she was the one who kept them running. She wanted to teach her kids to throw spirals and what a blitz was. She wanted to sit with Regan and Annabelle and Lacey and Priscilla in Football Mama T-shirts, and yell at the refs, and holler for their sons and watch their daughters cheer on the sidelines in Davis Karr Field. She wanted to attend every Valentine's Day dance from here on, and she wanted to be doing Cupid's Cock shots with the girls when she was eighty.

She didn't want New York or San Antonio. She wanted Bad.

And Nolan.

She wasn't sure what to do about that last part, but she did know that Bad was where she belonged. And she was not just okay with that, she was proud of that. She wasn't writing great novels or traveling the world or influencing the masses. But she was contributing to a town where good people were living good lives and were learning about and passing on things like love and community and loyalty and fun and the appreciation of the simple things. There was a lot of good going on in Bad. And it might be simple, *she* might be simple, but she was happy. She belonged here.

She looked at Teresa. "We're a blue-collar community. The world needs blue-collar communities. And I'm a part of that. The cars and trucks I work on help the people get to work and do their jobs," she said. She was taking a risk. She was taking on the biggest bitch in town. But just like the sixth-grade girls had been willing to come to blows over their team, Randi was willing to come to blows—verbal and otherwise—over her town. "The ranchers have to get out to their pastures and livestock. The truckers transport and bring back supplies. I keep the cop cars and the firetrucks and ambulances ready to go. I keep construction equipment running. I help the teachers and the nurses and the waitresses and everyone else get to work and to their jobs. They all contribute to this community, and to what the people from here turn out to be, whether it's ranching right there or becoming a lawyer in Shreveport. It's all important and we're all needed. Like the work *you* do."

Teresa's spine straightened and she narrowed her eyes. "What?"

"You contribute too. Dr. Weston has been the dentist here in Bad for forty years. He's a huge part of this town and everyone knows that his office would fall apart if it wasn't for you keeping things running. You're a part of his success."

Teresa crossed her arms tightly. "We work on teeth. It's not exactly saving the world."

"Well, I think the people who want to chew things would disagree," Randi said with a smile. "But you help keep the community healthy. You help them when they're in pain. And even more than teeth, Doc donates huge amounts of money to the rec program here, which helps keep the walking trail nice and the parks maintained and the baseball program going. All of that not only keeps us healthy, but gives people a lot of enjoyment. Without his successful practice, he wouldn't be able to do those things."

Randi took a breath. She was relieved Teresa wasn't arguing. Yet. So she went on. Into even more treacherous territory. "And," she said. "I know that you bring Dr. Weston lunch every day since his wife died because otherwise he would forget to eat. And you make sure he drinks something besides Coke all day."

"If he keels over, I'm out of a job," Teresa said.

Randi knew she should have expected something like that. But she smiled instead of sighing. Because she saw something important in Teresa's eyes—she liked what she was hearing.

Nolan had taught her over the past two weeks that sometimes having someone just say the words "you're great" or "I like you" could have a profound effect.

"Well, besides keeping Dr. Weston and the practice going, you bring up issues that need attention in Bad and keep us all on our toes."

Teresa snorted at that. "People hate when I show up at meetings."

Randi nodded. "Because you make them accountable for things."

"You think I'm doing a great job, bitching and moaning?"

Randi chose her words carefully. If she'd learned anything over the past two weeks, it was that words were very powerful. "I think you could approach it all differently, and maybe get more done because people would be more willing to listen. But yes, overall, I think it's great that you point out things that we should be aware of."

Teresa just looked at Randi. Her mouth was pinched and she looked a little suspicious. But she didn't look as suspicious as she had when they'd started talking. And she didn't look ready to slap Randi, so she counted that as a win.

"I like the white dress," Teresa finally said, dropping her arms and hitching her purse higher on her shoulder. "But you should wear the red shoes."

Then she turned and left.

Randi knew she was staring with her mouth open when Annabelle, Regan and Cilla came back into the changing area. Their mouths were all open too.

"Holy shit." Regan was the first one to speak. "That was... holy shit."

"I've never heard you talk like that," Annabelle told Randi. "That was amazing. You were so confident and used the exact right words."

Randi nodded. "Thanks." She looked at Cilla. "What do *you* think?"

Cilla held up a pair of strappy sandals with a three-inch heel. They were cherry red. "I think she's right about the shoes."

———

"The shoes stay on."

Nolan jerked his bow tie loose as he watched Randi turn. She had one hand braced on the back of the chair near the window and one foot off the floor. She was trying to undo the tiny buckle on the side of one red shoe.

"Oh really?" She gave him a sexy, knowing smile.

He stepped toward her. They weren't boots, but they were hot as hell. She was dressed completely inappropriately for February in New York, but she'd turned heads all night at the party. Nolan was pretty sure his own tongue had been hanging out all night. She looked like a princess...who was about to have a very charming screaming orgasm.

"But the dress can go. And the bra and panties."

He tossed his tie and jacket onto the bed and untucked his shirt.

The only thing about the night that had been good was Randi. She'd loved the trip to New York so far. She'd taken in the lights in Times Square with wide eyes, she'd laughed throughout the zig-zagging cab ride, she'd moaned in pleasure when she'd bit into the hot dog from the street vendor. She'd even said a soft "wow" when they'd stepped into the lobby of his editor's offices and then another one when they'd stepped off the elevator on the fortieth floor, where the party was being hosted.

"I'm not wearing a bra with this dress," she told him as she reached behind her for the zipper and pulled it down. The dress fell into a white cloud at her feet. She looked like an angel standing on that cloud. Bare-assed naked. "Or panties," she added.

"Come here."

He'd been wound up all night. In part because of the acres of peach-scented skin that had been flirting with the white dress that managed to look sweet and innocent and fuck-me-hard at the same time. Truly a case of heaven and hell for him.

The other part had been his editor. Who hated the new beginning chapters of his book.

Randi stepped out of the circle of the dress and walked toward him. Bare breasts, bare pussy, red heels—the best way to end the night. This was all he was going to focus on. This woman and the way she made him feel.

As soon as she got close enough, he tangled his hands in her hair, tipped her head and kissed her. Fucked her mouth, actually. He was not in the mood for sweet and slow and romantic. His emotions had been swirling ever since Brad had said, "What the hell was that?" about the new chapters, two seconds after handing Nolan a whiskey. At least he'd waited until Randi had disappeared into the ladies' room.

Nolan tamped those thoughts down and focused fully on the

hot, sweet mouth he was plundering with his tongue, and the noises she was making in response. Her hands fisted the front of his shirt, her heels put her three inches higher—lining her pelvis up with his almost perfectly.

He needed an outlet for all of this energy. The party hadn't been the you're-amazing celebration he'd expected from his editor and agent. He wasn't the only author in attendance, of course, and he was grateful they'd all had to spread their attention around. He hadn't wanted to spend the four hours talking about how he'd fucked up the book.

Randi's hands slid to his back and she pressed closer, and Nolan knew that she was the *only* thing that could take his mind off of the mess he'd created and wasn't sure he could fix.

He lifted his head and stared down at her dazed eyes and swollen mouth.

Randi. The only bright spot to all of this. Even if he'd screwed up the book completely, he wouldn't have traded the two weeks of conversation with her for anything.

"On the bed. Spread out."

She must have seen something in his eyes because she bit her bottom lip and then did exactly as she'd been told. She walked backward to the edge of the bed, sat down, then lay back, spreading her legs.

And Nolan couldn't even remember where they'd been ten minutes ago, not to mention the rest of the night before this moment.

He crossed to stand between her knees, drinking in the sight of her. "Damn, Randi."

"Touch me." She slid one knee up and let it fall to the side.

"I fully intend to. Over and over. All night long."

Randi moved her leg against the comforter. "When are you going to start?"

He felt his mouth curl. This woman wanting him was the best thing in his life. "Impatient?"

"I'm naked, spread out on your bed, and you're fully dressed and just standing there. I don't think it's impatient. I think it's horny."

He chuckled. And it was such a relief. The humor and the lust and the…love. All of the things that Randi made him feel were such a relief after the anger and resentment that had been balled in his gut all night.

"How about a 'please, Nolan, I'll die if you don't fuck me right now'?" he asked.

"I'm very prepared to stroke you, but I didn't realize it would be your ego."

He dragged a finger up her inner thigh. "Let's start with my ego. But we definitely won't stop there."

She gave him a heart-stopping grin. "Please, Nolan. I need you. I never realized how much another person could make me feel. But when I'm with you, I am the best version of myself and I feel like I can do anything."

His heart turned over in his chest. Holy… That was so much better than what he'd suggested.

"Now, *please* fuck me. I'll die if you don't."

Okay, it was *slightly* better. Because hearing her ask him to fuck her was pretty damned amazing too.

He didn't touch her again as he undressed. He'd planned to make this fast and dirty, something to completely block out the other thoughts and worries the night had stirred up. But he didn't need dirty. He just needed her. He had no thought in his head except making her feel everything she made him feel. And making her come. Hard.

He tossed his clothes to the side after fishing a condom out of his pocket. He rolled it on slowly, loving the way her pupils dilated and her tongue darted out to wet her lips as she watched.

"You ready for me, Ladybug?" he asked gruffly, giving himself an extra stroke or two.

"So ready."

Her voice was breathless and made his balls tighten.

"Show me." He didn't plan to say some of the things he said.

They just came out. But he wanted to see her touch herself suddenly as badly as he needed to breathe.

Randi didn't hesitate. She never did with him. It was as if she fully trusted him and was as wrapped up in what he was feeling as he was. She slid her hand down over her stomach to her mound, then over her clit. She gave a little moan as she did it. Then she kept going. Nolan had to stroke himself again to ease the ache. This wasn't going to last long.

Randi slid her middle finger into her pussy, moaning louder as she did it. She stroked in and out as he moved up and down his cock.

"Show me," he said again, his voice tight.

Her eyes locked on his, Randi pulled her finger out. It was glistening with wetness and his tongue tingled. He grasped her wrist and lifted her hand as he leaned in. He sucked her finger into his mouth, swirling his tongue over the length and taking all the sweetness from it.

"Need you," she told him huskily.

"Always," he said honestly. He would always need her.

He lined his cock up with her hot center and pressed forward, sliding into her slowly, his thumb rubbing over her clit. With her lying on the bed and him standing, the angle was excruciatingly perfect and he was able to stroke deep on the first glide.

They groaned together as she took him. He lifted her thighs, spreading her farther as he pulled out and then sank in again. He paused, balls deep, and just breathed.

"This," he finally said. "This is where I want to be forever."

"That will make it hard for me to go to work," she said, her voice catching as he moved in her.

"Don't care. Just want to be right here." He stroked deep, harder. "Right. Here." He thrust again. "Forever."

She arched her back, trying to get closer, but he had all the leverage. He pulled her against him as he thrust forward.

"*Yes.*"

"One of my favorite words," he said, doing it again.

"How about 'more'?" she asked.

"More? You've got all of me."

She gave him a sweet smile. "Yeah?"

"Absolutely. Every single part of me. Always."

"Then how about 'harder'?"

"That I can do." He thrust harder, deeper, faster.

Her body tightened around him, spurring him on, and her fingers curled into the comforter on either side of her hips.

He kept moving. Her breasts bounced, the noises she made got louder and higher, and he felt his climax coming.

"Play with your nipples, Randi," he commanded as he moved his thumb back to her clit and circled. "I need to feel you coming."

"I'm so close," she panted, moving a hand to her breast.

She took a tip between her thumb and finger, rolling, tugging, and he felt her inner muscles clench around him.

"Come on, Ladybug. Let me feel it. Let me see it."

Her breathing grew faster and he thrust harder. She continued playing with her nipple as he thumbed her clit and they climbed together toward their climaxes.

Finally he felt her pussy grab on and begin milking him as she cried out, his name on her lips. Nolan let go, pumping deep, filling her, and the moment after she broke, he felt his orgasm roar from the base of his spine, through his body and into hers.

He stood, making his lungs expand for a few moments before pulling her up and into his arms. He held her tight, his lips against her hair. "I love you, Randi. Love you so much."

She hugged him back, her face against his throat. "I love you too. No matter what."

———

Twenty minutes later, Randi was asleep, curled on her side with her sweet ass pressed against his hip.

Nolan was on his back, his arm under her, listening to her soft breathing, absorbing everything about the feeling of being with her like this. It could only be more perfect if they were in her bed in Bad. And if he wasn't going to have to leave her.

Fuck.

His editor's words wouldn't leave him alone. *What the hell was that?* Nolan gritted his teeth as Brad's voice replayed in his head. *This is supposed to be about football, not Mayberry. Hard-hitting, mud and guts and glory football. Remember? Those were your words.*

That was what Nolan had pitched when he'd pitched the book. That was what he'd intended to write. Sure, there was going to be inspiration and maybe some humor mixed in. This was Coach Karr after all. But the backbone of the book was supposed to be the hard work and the sacrifice and the digging deep that the game took—on the part of the Coach and the players.

Now the backbone of the book was Bad. The town, the people, the history.

Nolan loved it. He'd brought all of that to life, because of Randi.

And his editor hated it.

His agent was ticked off too. Typically, Hunter had Nolan's back. But this time he agreed with Brad. Neither thought the book was bad. In fact, they liked it. For a book about football in small-town Louisiana, it was excellent. But it wasn't the book they wanted. It wasn't the book they'd paid him a hundred thousand dollar advance for.

What got into you? Those had been Hunter's first words to him.

Then Hunter had gotten caught up in the story Randi was telling their little group about how the football mamas in Bad had suited up and played a game of flag football to raise money for the youth league—and how *flag* football had somehow resulted in a bloody nose, a sprained wrist and a lot of muddy uniforms. Everyone had laughed, including Randi, the sound light and happy, her face glowing and absolutely gorgeous.

Hunter had turned to Nolan with an eyebrow up and said, "Oh, I see what got into you."

Nolan felt his arm tense under Randi. She *had* gotten into him. He'd gone to her for help with the book and she'd given him exactly what he'd asked for—an appreciation for the game. He hadn't even realized he was looking forward to that first game in the fall until Hunter had said that. But yeah, she'd gotten into him.

So now…

Brad wanted the original book back. He wanted to go back to those first chapters and for Nolan to keep going. And he had one month. That was the last of the deadline extensions Brad was willing to give.

Hunter's advice had been, "Fucking write the book."

Nolan didn't want to write that book. He liked the new chapters. Hell, he liked all of the new chapters. But he recognized what was happening. His love for the new book was about his love for Randi. She was in every word, on every page. When he read over what he'd written, he could hear and see her in all of the stories.

So, he needed to leave her in Bad tomorrow—and head back to San Antonio and his apartment and his computer and block everything about her and Bad out and finish the fucking book.

———

Their wake-up call came at seven a.m. Randi rolled and stretched as Nolan grabbed the bedside phone, lifted the receiver and set it back down to stop the ringing.

He groaned.

She smiled.

It had been a late night, but it had been worth every milligram of caffeine she was going to need to mainline today.

New York City was amazing. She was happy she'd gotten to see it. She'd been amazed by the buildings and lights and *people*. She'd watched a half dozen street performers, given nearly fifty dollars away to homeless people, and been propositioned by two prostitutes, at the same time.

It was a fun, crazy, exciting place to be.

And she couldn't wait to get home. She loved seeing the city, dressing up, trying new things. But she was already ready to be home where nighttime was fully dark, where you could see farther than a city block at a time and where there was such a thing as quiet.

In fact, tonight she intended to sit on her back deck with a cold beer and look at the stars and listen to…absolutely nothing.

In her bare feet.

That was another thing she wasn't going to miss—it was damned cold in New York in February.

"You going to join me?" she asked Nolan from the doorway to the bathroom. She needed to take a shower, but it didn't have to be a fast shower.

He glanced at her and scrubbed a hand over his face. "Uh, no. You go ahead."

She frowned. He seemed distracted, and very tired. "You okay?"

"Yeah." He stood. "I'll order breakfast from room service."

"Okay, great." Randi couldn't explain it, but she felt cold all of a sudden.

But that was ridiculous. Everything was fine. He was tired and they'd had a big night last night. She knew he'd had a quick meeting with his editor when they'd first arrived. He probably just had a lot on his mind.

Randi showered and dressed and joined Nolan for breakfast at the little table in their room. But she'd just picked up a piece of bacon when he got to his feet and headed for the bathroom.

"Gonna shower."

She nodded and watched him go. Trepidation made the bacon not taste as good. Which was serious.

Nolan was quiet on the way to the airport and pulled out his laptop as soon as they were settled in the gate area.

Finally, she couldn't take it any longer. "What's going on?"

He looked up. "What?"

"You're quiet and distant. What happened? I thought the trip was good."

He looked back at his laptop. "I just have a lot of work to do."

"That's fine. I get it. But I don't love the silent treatment. Why not just say that?"

"I just have a lot on my mind."

She put a hand on top of his on the keyboard. "Talk to me. What happened at the party?"

He looked up, finally meeting her eyes. "I messed up the book. I didn't do the job. So I'm heading back to San Antonio tonight. I need to put my head down and work my ass off."

She frowned. He was leaving? Going back to San Antonio?

Of course he was. She'd known he would eventually. But she'd...yeah, maybe she'd been hoping that he would stick around awhile longer. He could write in Bad. He had been. He'd told her he'd gotten a lot done.

"I thought you were almost done with it," she said.

"I thought so too."

"Nolan, what happened?"

He sighed. "The book's not what they want."

"They don't want a book about Coach?"

"They want a book about Coach and football. What I gave them was a sappy book about a small town obsessed with football."

Randi felt the cold from earlier intensify. All the stories she'd told him. That's what they didn't like. "Oh. And staying in Bad—"

"Will make it worse."

Her throat tightened. "Oh."

"Clearly," he said with a frustrated sigh. "I let myself get all wrapped up in everything there, everything you told me about —in you—and I started to do my own thing and…" He shook his head. "I need to go home and get focused and get this done."

Randi felt her heart squeeze painfully. "Right. Sorry. I guess that was kind of my fault. I didn't stay on topic. Let me know if you need any help with the stuff you rewrite."

"Yeah." He looked like he was about to say more, but in the end he just said, "Okay."

"I'm—" She stopped and swallowed, rethinking her words for a moment. But then she went on. "I'm sorry that I distracted you from your work these past couple of weeks. You'd be a lot further ahead if you hadn't come home."

She'd said it to hear him deny it. She knew that. She also knew, looking into his eyes after she said it, that she should have kept her mouth shut. Because if he didn't deny it, it was going to hurt.

"Yeah, I would have."

Ouch.

"But It's my own fault. I didn't come to Bad to work on the book. And I should have left it alone. I should have gone home after a few days. I was the one who stuck around and started rewriting."

"You didn't come to Bad to work on the book?" she asked with a frown.

He gave yet another heavy sigh and shut his computer. "No, Randi, I came to Bad for you."

That sounded like something that should make her feel good. But it didn't. Everything about the way Nolan said that indicated he regretted it all.

She had nothing more to say. She nodded and stood. "I'm going to get some coffee."

She didn't come back to the gate until it was time to board. Nolan was typing furiously and he stopped only long enough to get on the plane. Randi took the window seat and stared out at the clouds, listening to the sound of Nolan's fingers on his keyboard all the way back to San Antonio.

She didn't let the tears fall until she was on the road back to Bad.

Nolan hadn't even argued with her about her plan to just rent a car to get home rather than having him drive her to Bad and then turn around to go back to San Antonio.

At least he'd kissed her goodbye.

CHAPTER NINE

EVERYTHING SUCKED.

Everything.

Even tequila. Maybe especially tequila. Because it reminded her of Nolan, and when she thought of Nolan, she got sad. And lonely. And horny.

It was *not* okay that tequila sucked.

The last time she'd been truly sad for several days at a time, it had been after the football team lost in district play. The last time she'd been lonely was...she couldn't even remember. The last time she'd been horny for days...had been after Nolan had kissed her at Coach's party.

She really wanted some tequila.

"What can I do?" Annabelle asked.

Randi felt the sting of tears as Annabelle took a seat on the overturned bucket where Nolan had spent so much time. That was so stupid. It was a bucket. She should have thrown it out. She should at least turn it over so people stopped sitting on it. Because every time they did, she had the urge to make them get up. It was Nolan's bucket. Which was definitely stupid. But it was also the reason she hadn't gotten rid of it.

"There's nothing. My life is over. I can't drink. I can't even part with a plastic bucket."

"Okay. A good attitude is everything," Annabelle said with a grin.

"My good attitude often comes from a glass bottle that says *tequila* on it. And now that makes me want to cry."

"You could talk to him."

Randi sighed. She couldn't. "Talking to him was what distracted him before. I'm trying to let him get his work done." And the thing was, she didn't really want to.

She understood he'd been stressed about the book and his editor not liking it. She got it. She understood getting caught up in work. There were times when she lost hours when she was under a car. But she hadn't heard from him in three weeks. Nothing. Not even an email. And that pissed her off.

He was the one who'd needed to work. Who'd needed to get back to San Antonio. Who had to put his head down. Fine. But when he lifted his head, he needed to be the one calling her.

And he hadn't.

"Randi! Someone here for you!" Luke called to her from the doorway to the main waiting area.

Randi looked over at him. "Who is it?"

"Someone who insists on having *you* look at his car."

Luke ducked back inside and the door shut behind him. She sighed. Seriously? She was so not in the mood for this. She didn't need picky customers today. Of course, she hadn't been in the mood for much over the past three weeks since she'd gotten back from New York. She wiped her hands on her rag.

"See you later?" she asked Annabelle.

"Of course." Annabelle stood from the bucket. "Want me to take this away with me?"

Randi started to say yes, please. But in the end, she shook her head. "No. Leave it."

Annabelle gave her a sympathetic look. "Okay."

Pathetic. She was completely pathetic. Maybe this next

customer would take her mind off of everything. Randi headed inside, trying to feel hopeful. But it was tough. She was destined to spend sixty hours a week in her garage for the rest of her life and her garage now reminded her of Nolan. For the rest of her life.

As Randi stepped into the waiting area and she saw who was there for her, she did, however, smile.

"Hey, Coach."

Coach Karr turned from where he was filling a cup with coffee. "Hey, Randi."

"How are you?" She crossed the room and lifted onto tiptoe to give him a kiss on the cheek. He was one of her favorite people and in spite of her crappy mood, she was happy to see him.

"Couldn't be better," Coach told her.

"Glad to hear it. So how's the car?" Randi asked Coach.

"Good."

She lifted an eyebrow. "Luke said you wanted me to look at it."

"Oh, right. Yep. Need new wiper blades," Coach said.

Now both her eyebrows went up. "You need me to replace your wiper blades?"

Coach sipped from his cup and nodded.

The man was one of the most intelligent people she knew. He crafted plays that made other coaches weep. He'd run his ranch for umpteen years. He'd raised a daughter all on his own. He'd been a father figure to dozens of young men. There was no way Davis Karr needed her to change his wiper blades. Something was up. And it was probably about Nolan.

Randi felt her heart squeeze at the thought of Nolan. He and Coach talked at least a couple times a month even when Nolan wasn't visiting. She was sure Coach knew that she knew that. He was waiting for her to ask about him. She sighed. If Coach had something to say that he thought she needed to hear, she was going to hear it. But she didn't have to encourage it.

"Okay," she said. "Pull the truck into bay three and we'll get you fixed up."

"Will do." Coach tossed his empty cup into the trash and headed for the front of the garage.

She watched him get into the truck and start it up. He was going to pretend he needed her to work on the truck rather than just getting to it?

Fine. She was going to charge him for the stupid blades.

He pulled into the bay and she grabbed the blade replacements from the store room. She climbed up on the running board and had the first one done in two minutes.

She moved to the other side to replace the second blade that was in practically perfect condition.

"Weather's been good, huh?" Coach asked.

For God's sake. They were going to talk about the weather? Literally?

Randi nodded. "It really has been."

"Heard you went to New York."

Now they were getting to it. She snapped the wiper back into place and jumped to the ground. "Yep."

She wasn't going to give him anything. If he wanted to know something specific, he could ask. This was Coach. He was a straight shooter. He told people what they needed to hear, whether they wanted to hear it or not. There was a reason he was working up to this. He was gauging her reactions and expressions. He was trying to read how she felt and what she was thinking. And he'd probably tell Nolan everything.

Well, she wasn't that easy.

"Cold up there, huh?" Coach asked.

"Yep. Very."

"Have a good time?"

"Yep. Very." She had. New York had been great. It was the stuff that came after that. "Okay, two new blades," she said. "You're all set."

"Will you check my wiper fluid while I'm here too?" Coach asked.

Wiper fluid? Really? Was there anyone who didn't know how to do that themselves? "Of course." She popped his hood.

"So how are you? Guess I didn't ask," he said as she filled up the nearly full fluid and replaced the cap.

"Fine. The same," she said, playing along. "Why do you ask?" There. She could be straightforward if he couldn't.

"Just checking on one of my favorite girls."

She gave him a legitimate smile. "You're sweet."

Just say what you have to say.

"How's the coolant?"

Okay, fine. She checked. "Looks good."

"And the brake fluid?"

She checked. "Yep, you're good."

"How about the tire pressure?"

She sighed. What was going on? Why not just say what he'd come here to say? She pulled the pressure gauge from her back pocket and squatted next to the passenger side front tire.

The pressure was perfect. As expected. She moved to the back tire. Also fine.

Finally, she caved. "You really going to have me check them all?" she asked.

"Yep. And the oil, the filters, the hoses."

She got to her feet. "Which will all be perfectly fine."

"Probably."

She turned and tucked her hands into her back pockets. "What's going on?"

"I've been waiting for you to come to me for at least two weeks."

"About?"

"Nolan."

She gave him a little smile, but her chest hurt just hearing his name out loud. "Why did you think I would come to you about him?"

"Because you're in love with him and he's acting like a jackass."

She gave a short laugh. "You can help with that?"

"Oh, I'm a specialist in dealing with jackasses," he said. "Lots of practice."

She smiled, but shook her head. "He had to go back to San Antonio to finish the book." She swallowed hard. "I distracted him too much."

Coach gave her a half smile. "Well, that's as it should be. If a man isn't distracted by the woman he loves, he's doing something wrong."

Her heart kicked at hearing Coach say Nolan was in love with her. She believed it, actually. But hearing someone else acknowledge it felt...awesome.

She shrugged. "He tried working here. The distraction thing ruined the book."

Coach shook his head. "Not possible."

"I promise you, that's exactly what happened. The book he wrote while he was with me isn't the one his editor wanted."

"Oh, well, that's different from ruined," Coach said. "The things a person does when they're in love are the best things they ever do. Especially when it comes to being creative. How do you think romance novels and love songs and poetry happen? Without love, the most beautiful things in the world would have never been created."

She shook her head, but couldn't help her smile. She loved this guy. He was one of the toughest men she'd ever met. He could chew ass, yell, and rant better than anyone. She'd seen him yell at a ref, one inch from the other guy's nose. She'd seen him throw clipboards, water jugs, helmets and a hundred other things halfway across a football field. But he was also one of the sweetest, most loving men she knew. Because he got people. He really got them. And he always believed the best of them.

"He's in San Antonio, finishing the book, because he's obligated to do it," she said. "He has a contract and he's not the type to back out. He made a promise to them and he'll honor that. And he has to be there, because when he's here with me, he wants to write something...different. I understand."

"You understanding doesn't mean he shouldn't apologize to you."

She swallowed. "Yeah. Maybe."

"I want you to know, if you realized you didn't really love him when you saw how he acts under pressure, I get it."

Randi straightened away from the car. "No. That's not it. I do love him. He was a jerk, but that doesn't change the way I feel about him."

"But he hasn't said he's sorry."

"No. But..." She didn't have an excuse for him. "No, he hasn't."

Coach nodded. "He will."

"You think so?"

"Yeah, cuz I'm gonna chew his ass and tell him to."

Randi shook her head. "You can't do that. He has to mean it."

"Oh, honey," Coach said, putting his hand on top of her head. "If I didn't know he'd mean it, I wouldn't tell him to do it."

Randi pulled in a deep breath. "Okay."

"Good." Coach pulled his keys from his pocket and started around to the driver's side of the truck.

He opened the door and Randi shook herself. "What? You came over here today and went through all of that just to tell me he was going to be apologizing?"

Coach turned back, his hand gripping the edge of the door. "No. I came over here to let you know that I love you for loving a jackass and that I know that ain't easy."

She smiled in spite of herself. "You didn't tell me that."

"But you know it anyway, right?"

She nodded. "Yeah."

He gave her a wink and got into his truck. But before he shut the door she called, "Those wiper blades aren't free you know."

"How much?" he asked with a grin.

She ran her gaze over the car. "Three hundred and fifty-two and thirty-one cents."

He chuckled. "Wow."

"That's twelve thirty-one for the blades, forty for labor and three hundred for annoying me."

He nodded. "Put it on my bill."

She laughed and he got up into the truck. Just before he started the engine, she said, "Hey, Coach?"

"Yeah?"

"Thanks."

"For what?"

"Chewing the jackass's ass."

"Like I said, I'm kind of a specialist."

"And be sure to tell him I love him."

Coach nodded. "Right after I tell him that if he doesn't already know that, he's also a dumbass."

Then he gave her a wink and drove off, wiping his windshield with his new wipers.

———

"I can't believe you haven't been back here in a *month*."

Nolan sighed. "Hi, Mom."

Teresa set her purse on the kitchen counter. She wasn't surprised to see him—Nolan had called to tell her he was on his way this morning—but she didn't look thrilled to see him either.

"And you ate the pie?"

Nolan looked down at the empty pie plate in front of him on his mother's kitchen table. "I've been eating microwave burritos and frozen pizza for the past month. I couldn't help it."

Teresa shook her head and moved to the refrigerator, and Nolan knew she was about to make him a sandwich. He didn't even think about trying to stop her. He was certainly old enough to make his own sandwich, but somehow Teresa's always tasted better.

He wasn't sure he could ever look at another burrito as long as he lived.

But instead of sandwich ingredients, Teresa took eggs, butter and milk out.

Maybe she was going to make him an omelet. That would work too.

"I'm just saying that a *month* is a really long time," Teresa said, pulling the canisters of flour and sugar from the cupboard.

So not an omelet. Maybe more pie. He could be okay with that.

"I know a month is a long time, Mom." It had been a month since he'd seen Randi too. A horrible month. Thirty days of fighting, on a nearly hourly basis, the urge to drive to Bad, fall at Randi's feet and beg her to just let him sit in her shop and watch her work and talk to her.

He knew very well how fucking long that was. He was going crazy. But he had to do this right.

"I can't believe you let her drive herself back to Bad. After telling her that she was the reason your book ended up sucking."

Nolan loved and hated his mother's hair salon. There wasn't a single secret about anything in Bad because of that place. When it came to finding out news about his old friends, and yes, Randi, he'd loved it. But damn, having his own stupid mistakes spread all over town was irritating. Clearly Randi had confided in her friends. Who had confided in other friends, who had told someone else, who had told someone else.

"Mom," Nolan said firmly. "I did not tell her the book sucked because of her. The book didn't—doesn't—suck, for one thing. And it wasn't her fault. It was me. I was the one that got sidetracked. And I know a month is a long time. Too long. Okay? But I had to do it. I had to finish the book. It was…she was…I didn't have a choice."

Teresa broke eggs into a bowl and added the sugar and

butter. "You could have forgotten the book. You could have told your editor to shove it. You could have chosen *her* over your work."

Nolan opened his mouth, but she turned on the mixer, the whirring of the beaters too loud to be heard.

He waited until she'd stopped it to say, "Are you telling me that you think I should have given up my book deal, paid back my huge advance, turned my back on the career that has made you incredibly proud, that is everything you wanted for me, so that I could come back and stay here with Randi?"

Teresa got the baking soda, salt and other ingredients out of the cupboard and started measuring things into the bowl. But she did answer. "Yes."

Nolan frowned at her back. "What the hell are you talking about?"

Teresa stirred the contents of her bowl for a few seconds. "I'm talking about..." Teresa took a breath and shook her head. "I'm talking about maybe I was wrong."

Nolan blinked. He didn't think he'd ever heard his mother say the words I, was, and wrong, together in a row.

"What's going on?" He narrowed his eyes. "Are you okay? Are you sick? Do you have a fever?"

Teresa set her spoon down and turned. "No, I'm not okay, Nolan. My son hasn't returned a call to me in a month. The only contact I've had is an email once a week that said "I'm working. I'm fine" and then the email with your book attached. You walked away from a girl who, by all counts, is miserable without you. You walked away from a girl that you're in love with, presumably making you equally miserable. You became a hermit for a month to write a book that you hate. Then I walk in here to find you looking like hell and that you've eaten the pie I need for later this afternoon. So no, I'm not okay."

Nolan processed all of that. She was right on pretty much every count. "I don't hate the book," he said. "It turned out great. And I'm not *equally* miserable. I'm way *more* miserable than she could possibly be."

But the rest was true. He'd become a hermit. He'd walked away from Randi—or at least he'd let *her* drive away from *him*. He hadn't talked to his mom, or anyone else, for a month. And he did look like hell. He *felt* like hell.

Teresa nodded. "Good."

"Good?"

"If you weren't more miserable than she is, I would worry that you're more like your dad than I thought."

Being like his dad was the ultimate cut down from Teresa. Nolan frowned at her. "You were thinking I was like dad?"

"I worried for a little while," she admitted. "He was able to walk away and forget everything here."

Nolan swallowed. "What made you stop worrying?"

"I remembered how you looked at her at the Valentine's Day dance," Teresa said.

Nolan shifted his weight. "How did I look at her?"

"Like you never wanted to be anywhere else."

That hit Nolan hard in the chest. He knew how his mother felt about this. But it was time to make her understand. He was home. In Bad. To stay. "You're right," he said. "I never want to be anywhere but with Randi."

Teresa nodded. "Your dad never looked at me like that."

Nolan felt his heart squeeze. "I…I'm sorry, Mom."

She shrugged. "That's harder to find than you think."

Nolan nodded. "That's why I want to be sure to hang on to it."

"Good." She gave him a sincere smile. "And now it will be okay. You're finally back and you're not leaving again."

Nolan frowned. "You're *glad* that I'm back here in Bad and not leaving?"

Teresa nodded. "Yes."

"They have great medications now that can help with multiple personalities, you know."

"Nolan?"

"What?"

"Be nice or I won't help you win Randi back."

"You're going to have to tell me what changed your mind about all of this," he said. He was happy for her change of heart, of course, but he was also very curious about it. "But first tell me how you're going to help me win her back."

Teresa gave him a grin, unlike any he'd ever seen from his mother before. "I have an idea."

"Great. I'm all ears."

"Well, tell me where you most want to propose to her."

Nolan felt his eyebrows shoot up. "Propose?"

"You *are* going to propose to her, right?"

"Well…"

"Nolan."

"Yes. I was thinking about proposing." He paused. "You're going to *help me* propose to Randi?"

Teresa straightened. "Randi is a wonderful person and you should grab her and marry her and never let her go."

"You know when I say Randi, I mean Miranda Doyle? The cute mechanic. The one that you said wasn't good enough for me a few weeks ago."

Teresa frowned at him. "I'm starting to wonder if *you're* good enough for *her*, frankly."

"Is that right?" Nolan was thrilled, of course. But this was interesting, to say the least.

"It is right. And let me tell you something else, Nolan Phillip Winters," Teresa said. "If you're going to live in this town and just sit around and write books and columns, then you're going to need to give some money to community projects or volunteer for some committees or something. You need to give back. We're all a part of the people and things that come out of this town."

Nolan was definitely going to get this story later. But right now, he needed to find Randi. He crossed to his mother and pulled her into his arms. "I love you, Mom. And I would like to have a doctor give you a full psychological workup. But I will give money and time to whatever you ask me to. Now will you please tell me your idea for how I can get Randi back?"

He thought he heard a sniff, but he had to be wrong. Teresa Winters didn't cry.

"Yes. Let me finish these cookies and I'll tell you all about it." But she squeezed him before letting him go.

"Cookies?" He moved back to the table and sat down to the last three bites of pie.

"Someone ate the pie I made." Teresa got busy with her cookie dough again.

"Why do you need to have sweets?"

"Because I have friends coming over for coffee later."

Nolan swallowed his bite of pie hard. "You...do?"

"Yes."

"You and Monica were going to eat a whole pie?" As far as Nolan knew, Monica Williams was the only friend Teresa had.

"I have more friends."

"Since when?"

"Since about a month ago."

He wanted to ask her how. He loved his mother, but he knew she wasn't the most popular woman in town. Instead he asked, "Why?"

"Because someone helped me see that being a part of something can be pretty great, and once I started looking around, I realized I *am* a part of things here. And I decided to try to enjoy it instead of resenting it."

"I...um. Wow."

She looked over her shoulder at him. "It's amazing what you miss when you don't call or visit for so long, huh?"

Apparently.

"We have some catching up to do," he admitted. "But we have a lot of time now. I'm here to stay."

Teresa beamed at him. "Let's talk about how to get Randi to

say yes. You're going to need something big. Because it's been a *month*."

Nolan sighed. "Yes, Mom, I know."

"Fuck this."

Randi looked around the hood of the car she was working on to see Priscilla standing there, hands on her hips.

"Are you okay?" Randi asked.

"No. I'm kinda pissed, actually." Cilla walked straight to Randi, took her hand and pulled her toward the door to the waiting area.

Now what? Coach had left about three hours ago and Randi had been thinking about their conversation ever since. It was past closing and everyone was gone, making this the best place to think.

"What's up?" Randi asked, following her friend.

"Girls' Night. And you're coming. But there are some rules tonight."

"Rules?"

Cilla stopped by the small office where she knew Randi kept her personal belongings while she worked.

"Yes. Go in, change your clothes and meet me out here in ten minutes. We're going to Bad Brews and we're getting tequila, and you're not going to cry, you're not going to leave early and we are, by God, making this a *great* night with lots of fun so that you can get back to liking tequila. And your life."

Randi appreciated the gesture. "I just—"

"I'm not asking," Cilla told her with a firm look. "All the girls are there. Let's go."

Randi looked back at the car she hadn't even really been working on, then at her friend. The women at Bad Brews had been here for her for so long and, more importantly, would continue to be here for her. They were going to grow old together. Sure, Priscilla and Annabelle and Regan and Bailey and the others were madly in love. But they were still going to be having girls' nights when they were eighty. They would be there with emergency chocolate anytime she called. They were going to be sharing her blanket, and her spiked cider, at football games until they were too old to climb into the bleachers. And then they were going to line their lawn chairs up by the fence like the old ladies did now. They deserved her time and attention and energy. She wanted tequila to make her think of her friends, not Nolan.

"Yeah, okay. Let's do it. We're going to make tequila fun again," Randi decided. She pulled the ponytail holder out of her hair as she headed into the office. "Let me grab a clean shirt and my boots." She always kept extra clothes and shoes in the office for just such an occasion. These occasions actually came up quite a bit.

She changed quickly and soon they were walking through the door to Bad Brews.

The place was packed and Randi took a deep breath. This was home. Every single inch of this place was familiar and filled with memories. The people here were *her* people. The music was her music. And she wouldn't trade this for any party in New York or even Paris. This was where she belonged.

The feeling of comfort washed over her and she happily followed Priscilla to their table, where Annabelle, Regan and the rest of their gang were already sitting. Bailey arrived with a tray full of shot glasses the moment Randi's butt hit the chair.

"Glad to see you," she said with a wink.

"Here's to making tequila fun again," Cilla said, lifting her glass.

Randi joined in the toast and shot back the drink. It burned in its old familiar way and she found herself smiling. Did it make her miss Nolan? Sure. But would she have skipped over the tequila body shots if she'd known how things were going to go? No way.

"Another," Randi said, and all the girls cheered.

They followed up with beer and girl talk and laughing and thirty minutes later, Randi was feeling a lot more like her old self. Comfortable. Happy. Where she belonged.

That feeling lasted another three seconds.

"Randi."

Randi watched her friends' eyes widen just before she turned. Slowly. With butterflies swooping in her stomach.

Teresa Winters was behind her.

"Um, hi, Teresa."

"Hi." The older woman gave her a big smile. "I have something for you. I was going to bring it to the shop but someone stopped by the house and I didn't get a chance to get there before you left."

Randi straightened. "You have something for me?"

Teresa nodded and pulled a wrapped rectangle out of her big purse. She handed it to Randi, but when Randi tried to take it, Teresa kept hold of it.

"Do you love my son?" Teresa asked.

Randi didn't answer right away. She took a deep breath, wet her lips. Breathed again. But then she couldn't help it. She missed him, she was angry with him, she was hurt. But she couldn't deny how she felt.

"Yes."

"Good." Teresa let go of the package.

Randi knew what it was immediately. It was a book. "Um, is this from Nolan?"

Teresa nodded.

Randi swallowed. *The* book. The reason he'd pushed her away. "I don't—"

"Just look at it."

Randi lifted her eyes to Teresa's. "I love him. But I don't know if things will work out."

"I know. And going back to San Antonio was a crappy thing

to do. If it's any consolation, it might be the first crappy thing he's ever done."

Randi actually laughed at that. Of course Teresa thought that. But Randi had to admit she might have a point. "I'm not sure that I'm consoled knowing that I'm the reason he was crappy for the first time."

Teresa smiled. "I know how that sounds."

Randi just nodded, her gaze dropping to the wrapped book. Even without looking at it, the book was making her heart pound and her stomach twist.

"I really think you want to see this," Teresa said, her voice gentler now.

She was going to unwrap it. If nothing else, because Teresa Winters had started opening up in the past month—she smiled at people when she passed them on the street, she'd actually skipped the last Chamber of Commerce meeting, and rumor had it that she'd started a book club, inviting a few other women her age over for coffee and book talk, and even baking for them. Their first selection had been Nolan's first book, of course, but they had since read Michelle Obama's *Becoming*, and a couple of romances.

So Randi would look at the book because Teresa had brought it to her.

But damn, she didn't want to.

She'd seen the cover for the book on Amazon and had teared up. The photo was of the Renegades field at night, taken through the uprights, with the tall lights shining brightly. *Upright* was already selling well in the pre-order period, and when she'd read the first few pages that they showed online, she'd had a hard time breathing. The dedication read *To Coach. Because no one writes books about guys who play it safe.*

Finally she took a deep breath and ripped the wrapping paper off.

But it wasn't the book Nolan had written about Coach Karr in her hands.

This book was also by Nolan. It also featured a photo of the Renegades field, but this one had the players huddled up in the center of the field, the stands full of their fans behind them.

It was called *The Boys of Fall*.

Randi looked up at Teresa. "What is this?"

"His other book."

"*Other* book?"

"He wrote it at the same time he was finishing *Upright*. He's self-publishing this one. And that is the first copy. It goes on sale tomorrow."

Randi didn't know what to say. She turned the book over.

The Boys of Fall. A collection of essays about small-town football—the victories, the defeats, and the fans that make it all matter.

Randi swallowed hard.

"These are the stories we've told him," Teresa said. "All the people he interviewed, behind the scenes stuff, but..."

Randi looked up.

"But mostly the stuff you told him," Teresa said. "The stories that made him love football. And you."

Randi shook her head. "He doesn't love football."

"He loves Bad football. Now. Because you helped him see that very little of it is actually about the game. And you helped him know all of us better. You helped *me* know everyone better."

"Really?"

"I got to beta read the book. He figured I'd be the harshest critic of anything about Bad." She shrugged. "I liked it."

Randi breathed deep, her eyes stinging.

"Read the dedication," Teresa said, opening the front cover.

"Oh my God, read it out loud," Annabelle said.

The words blurred and Randi had to blink. She finally shook her head. "You read it." She handed the book to Annabelle.

"Out loud," Regan added, leaning onto the table eagerly.

Annabelle cleared her throat. "The fifty is where anything can happen, things can go either way, and it's all about who wants it more. It's all about possibilities and desire at the fifty. Miranda Doyle."

Randi felt her heart thump and a tingling start at her scalp and travel to her toes.

Annabelle and Regan looked at her, their eyes huge.

"You said that?" Priscilla asked.

Randi nodded.

"Wow, that's really good," Annabelle said.

Randi chuckled in spite of the swirl of emotions going through her. "Thanks." She looked at the book. "I can't believe he used that."

"And I'm not done reading," Annabelle said.

Randi sat up straighter. "Okay, go on."

"He signed it," Annabelle said. "And it's amazing."

"Read it," Regan said, almost bouncing in her seat.

"It says, To Miranda, M—"

Randi grabbed the book.

"Noooo!" Regan protested.

But Randi could barely hear her because she was reading Nolan's words.

To Miranda, Marry Me.

"Come *on*," Regan said.

Randi handed it to her.

"Oh my God!" Regan looked up at her.

"I know," Randi answered.

"But...oh my God!"

"I know."

"So how do you say yes?" Annabelle asked, looking around. She focused on Teresa. "Is he coming? Is he hiding somewhere?"

Teresa looked at Randi. "You know what to do."

She did. "Okay."

"What?" Regan asked, looking back and forth between them. "What's happening?"

"I have to go," Randi said, sliding off the stool.

"*What?*" Annabelle asked. "Where?"

"Can we come?" Priscilla asked.

Randi laughed, the truth of the situation finally fully sinking in and the joy bubbling up. Coach had known about this. He had to. He'd come to be sure she was in the right place emotionally to accept it. Either that, or he was magically able to just *know* when someone needed to talk to him.

That was entirely possible too. Randi had always thought he had a magic touch.

"This is kind of a private thing," she told her friends.

"I want to see him get on his knee!" Priscilla said.

"I want to see you say yes!" Annabelle added.

Randi laughed and grabbed her purse. "I'll tell you all about it later."

They both slumped in their seats.

"Well, at least come back for celebratory tequila," Regan said. "*That* should make you like it again."

"Okay, but Christopher might not like you sucking tequila out of my belly button. That's how Nolan and I do it," Randi said, feeling lighter than she had in a month.

Regan grinned, then laughed. "Oh, I think Christopher might like that a lot."

"Come to think of it, I could use some tequila and belly button practice," Annabelle said, waving Bailey over to the table. "I'm going to need a bottle of tequila to go."

"Make that two," Priscilla said.

Bailey already had one in hand. And a lime. She grabbed the salt shaker off the table and passed it all over to Randi. "I'm sick of you not liking my tequila anymore."

Randi lifted an eyebrow. "How did you know that this—"

"It's a small town," she said with a shrug.

"A small town that knows what goes on in my living room when I'm there alone with my boyfriend?"

Bailey nodded. "Yeah, when your boyfriend is good friends with *our* boyfriends."

Randi didn't care one bit that everyone in town knew about

the tequila shots. Or about anything else at this moment other than getting to Nolan.

"Go get him, girl," Bailey said.

Randi took a deep breath, gave her friends a smile and turned toward the door.

Teresa stopped her. "Thank you for loving my son."

Randi felt her throat tighten. "I can't help it."

Teresa smiled and stepped out of the way.

Ten minutes later, Randi walked through the short tunnel that led from the parking lot to Davis Karr Field.

Nolan was sitting on the fifty yard line, legs outstretched, leaning back on his hands.

She didn't miss a step.

When she got to midfield, she stopped. "You thought you could get me back with just some pretty words?"

He looked up. "Um, yeah. I'm good with words."

"Yeah. You are. It would have been nice to have a few of those over the past month."

He nodded. "Yeah. I know." He swallowed. "I'm really sorry. I just… I honestly kept thinking that I'd find a stopping place and I'd call you, and then I wasn't sure what to say until I could tell you I was done and coming home. And then when I was done and coming home, I just wanted to get here. And tell you in person." He looked miserable. And sorry. "But you are in every word of that book, Randi. Writing it made me fall in love with you all over again."

"It's been a *month*," she said.

"I know."

"So you're going to have to do better than words." She was lying. His words were exactly what she needed. Like how much he loved her. How amazing he thought she was. And that he wanted to marry her.

But she handed him the tequila and the lime, then stripped off her shirt and stepped forward, her feet on either side of his knees. She sank down onto his lap.

He gave her a smile that was filled with joy, love and amusement. "Tell you what, I'll show you with *actions*, but I'm going to need some words from *you*."

She wrapped her arms around his neck. "Oh yeah? Words? As in plural?"

His big hands went to her back and he brought her in until their lips almost touched. "You're right. I really only need one."

"Ye—"

"But let me say a few first," he cut her off.

She leaned back, unable to hide her smile. But she nodded. "Okay."

"I'm sorry. I was wrong about the book and the stories you told me. Those might not have been what New York wanted, but they are what *I* wanted to write about. They *made* the book that I wanted to write. And that's the kind of book I want to keep writing. About people and relationships and connections. I have more ideas and I'm going to keep going with them. From right here in Bad. And I love you. You're amazing and I want to spend every day of my life making sure you know that. I want to be with you forever. Here, in Bad. Forever."

Her heart was thundering, and she wanted nothing more than to wrap herself around him and just *be* with him. But she nodded. "Good."

"And, I just..." He trailed off.

He just sat looking at her for several long moments.

Finally she tipped her head. "What?"

"I can't believe it, but I'm out of words," he told her with a small laugh. "I guess that's all I needed to say."

Her heart expanded in her chest, and she realized that she had never loved anyone, and never would love anyone, the way she loved him. "So it's my turn?" she asked.

"I guess so."

"Okay." She took a big breath. "Yes."

A smile spread slowly, but it was huge and bright by the time he pulled her in and kissed the hell out of her.

When they finally came up for air, he said, "I have one more word for you after all."

"Okay."

He tipped her over onto the grass on the fifty-yard line on the Renegades football field and followed her down. "Tequila."

Thank you so much for reading Nolan and Randi's story! There's a lot more sexy, fun from Bad!

These books are all standalones and don't need to be read in any particular order!

The Best Bad Boy: (Jase and Priscilla)
A bad boy-good girl, small town romance

Bad Medicine: (Brooke and Nick)
A hot boss, medical, small town romance

Bad Influence: (Marc and Sabrina)
An enemies to lovers, road trip/stuck together, small town romance

Bad Taste in Men: (Luke and Bailey)
A friends to lovers, gettin'-her-groove back, small town romance

Not Such a Bad Guy: (Regan and Christopher)
A one-night-stand, mistaken identity, small town romance

Return of the Bad Boy: (Jackson and Annabelle)
A bad boy-good girl, fake relationship, small town romance

Bad Behavior: (Carter and Lacey)
A bad boy-good girl, second chance small town romance

Got It Bad: (Nolan and Randi)
A nerd-tomboy, opposites attract, small town romance

Find all of my books at
ErinNicholas.com

ͻ
And join in on all the FAN FUN!

Join my **email list!**
bit.ly/Keep-In-Touch-Erin
(be sure you get those dashes and capital letters in there!)

And be the first to hear about my news, sales, freebies, behind-the-scenes, and more!

Or for even more fun, join my **Super Fan page** on Facebook and chat with me and other super fans every day! Just search Facebook for Erin Nicholas Super Fans!

WANT MORE FROM THE BAYOU?

There's so much more from Erin's Louisiana bayou world!

Head down the road to Autre next and dive into the Boys of the Bayou series (where you'll first meet the Landry family)!

All available now!

My Best Friend's Mardi Gras Wedding

Sweet Home Louisiana

Beauty and the Bayou

Crazy Rich Cajuns

Must Love Alligators

Four Weddings and a Swamp Boat Tour

———

And be sure to check out **the connected rom com series,**

Boys of the Bayou-Gone Wild

Otterly Irresistible

Heavy Petting

Flipping Love You

Sealed With A Kiss

Say It Like You Mane It

Head Over Hooves

Kiss My Giraffe

———

And the **Badges of the Bayou** (where you get to know Michael LeClaire and JD Evans!)

Gotta Be Bayou

Bayou With Benefits

Rocked Bayou

Stand Bayou

Stuck Bayou

Just Wanna Be Bayou

———

And MUCH more—

including my printable booklist— at

ErinNicholas.com

ABOUT ERIN

Erin Nicholas is the New York Times and USA Today bestselling author of over forty sexy contemporary romances. Her stories have been described as toe-curling, enchanting, steamy and fun. She loves to write about reluctant heroes, imperfect heroines and happily ever afters. She lives in the Midwest with her husband who only wants to read the sex scenes in her books, her kids who will never read the sex scenes in her books, and family and friends who say they're shocked by the sex scenes in her books (yeah, right!).

Find her and all her books at
www.ErinNicholas.com

And find her on Facebook, Goodreads, BookBub, and Instagram!

Ingram Content Group UK Ltd.
Milton Keynes UK
UKHW011900310323
419486UK00005B/525